Before I Let Go

How Far Do You Go to Keep Your Soulmate?

Before I Let Go

How Far Do You Go to Keep Your Soulmate?

Steven "Chris" Ware

Copyright

ISBN-13: 978-1-947656-37-6

ISBN10: 1947656376

The Butterfly Typeface Publishing
PO BOX 56193
Little Rock Arkansas 72215

Dedication

This book is dedicated to my Grandma Norene:

You got to see the child that I was.

You never got to see the boy I was starting to become,

but I know you are looking down on the man that I am.

Rest in Peace

"A man will use a woman to feel like the king of his castle, but he won't necessarily make that woman his queen."

Steven "Chris" Ware

Table of Contents

Foreword

When I was in grade school, I loved to read. Our homeroom teacher would take us to the library and I would always pick out a couple of the *Encyclopedia Brown* mystery books by Donald J. Sobol.

By middle school, I lost interest in reading because of the required material and subsequent book reports. I considered those books to be boring. However, in the tenth grade, we were required to read a book called Durango Street by Frank Bonham and again I found myself in love with reading. That book renewed my interest in reading and from then on I read on a regular basis.

Fast forward to 1995, I had just saw the movie trailer for *Waiting to Exhale.* I got the book because I wanted to read it before the movie came out. I loved that book, so I went and bought two more books of Terry McMillan.

After a few years of reading books written by black women, I decided I needed to hear a different perspective. In my opinion, the books written by women had a lot of male bashing in them. I wanted to hear what we (black men) had to say!

The books I read by men seem to be written with women in mind and again in my opinion, they were offering more of the same in regards to male bashing.

That's when my cousin, Ms. Latosha Ware, recommended I read this book called *Milk In My Coffee* by Eric Jerome Dickey. Finally, a book written to appeal to both genders.

I thought to myself, "I can do this too." I wasn't sure if I would be good at it, but I knew I had a voice that people would want to hear.

So, I started putting my thoughts on paper.

Those thoughts eventually became stories, and those stories became this novel you are about to read.

I love reading. I love writing. And I know that you will love what I have to say!

Steven "Chris" Ware

Acknowledgments

I can't believe I'm writing the dedication and
acknowledgements
for a published book that I wrote!

Yep I'm grinning as I type this. Lol!
For those of you close to me, you have been waiting on
this for a while.
I finally did it!

I want to begin by thanking God for blessing me with
this talent.
I would like to thank the late Earnest Pool Jr. and the
lovely Thelma Ware-King
for giving me LIFE.
Much love to Theotis King for being my daddy and
showing me how to live LIFE.

Brandi Crew-Ware: The love of my LIFE, thank you for
making my LIFE worth living!

I've got to show some love and thanks to my other
mother and sponsor,
Mrs. Felicia Thompson.

Much love to my homie, my Ace, Jonathan Hart for
always believing in me.
For years you told me to 'get your stuff out there!'

A big shout out to Alex Ware, Vincent Brown, Brandon
Bonds, Ezekiel Williams,
Anthony Sims and Marcus Eagles; your encouragement
was needed & appreciated.

To the special ladies who for years gave me positive
feedback & constructive criticism:
my sister Katrina King, Tonya Banks, Tongela Allen,
Pamela Royal, Brittany Hood,
Keisha Lewis, Wendy Jones, Tracy Grant, Toya Hampton
and Sharonda Randle.
Ladies I can't say thank you enough, so thank you, thank
you, thank you.

XOXO to all my extended family and friends who I didn't
call by name.
I love and appreciate you too!

Last but not least, I want to thank Iris M. Williams and
Butterfly Typeface Publishing
for believing in me.
I always knew I had a voice that needed to be heard,
thank you for giving me the microphone!

Steven "Chris" Ware

Jason

Like Peas and Carrots

I was in a period of transition. The ink on my divorce papers were barely dry. Sitting at the bar at Club Matrix, my mind was everywhere. A sexy chick was at the other end of the bar. I noticed she kept looking my way with a smile on her face, flirting from a short distance. I was wearing a white Ralph Lauren polo with a black sports coat, and expensive jeans made by the same Bronx designer. She couldn't keep her eyes off this 6'4" brotha with the medium brown skin and deep dimples.

But as fine as she was I stayed on my end of the bar. This divorcee wasn't ready to get back in the dating game right now.

As always, my homies were late, so I was alone waiting on them to help me celebrate my new freedom. Celebrating freedom was their idea, I was drinking this liquid courage to hide my pain. The pain of knowing my family was broken. Two shots of Jose Cuervo and half of this Long Island tea had given me a good buzz. My marriage was over 2 years after Monica and I stood before God, family and friends. We stood in front of everybody and said we'd be together in sickness and health, for richer or poorer, or until we died. Hell, it was that 'for poorer' shit that got us.

I was a high school basketball coach and Monica was the prettiest girl in law school. With only one income, money was tighter than a virgin on Sunday morning. But we were ok, at least I thought we were. We ate every day, the lights or the phone was never disconnected. We even had cable, and everyone knows that when money is tight the cable is usually the first to go.

Problem was, we didn't have the money for elaborate vacations, shopping sprees, or for going out to eat every weekend, and all the other things she thought she needed to be happy.

I was content with our situation, because I could see the light at the end of the tunnel.

I knew once she passed the bar and started working, we were going to be fine. Slowly but surely things would get better. But for her, our money struggles were too stressful, stressful enough to make her cry on another man's shoulder. She went from his shoulder to his bedroom pillow.

She passed the bar and was gone before she tried her first case.

Now I'm here, drowning my sorrows with papers folded away in my sports coat, outlining visitation rights and child support payments concerning Nyia Nicole Hart, my 5-year-old daughter, my sunshine on a cloudy day. Damn I feel so lame, half drunk, sitting here quoting song lyrics from the Motown era.

I grew up with both my parents. My baby girl wasn't supposed to be raised like this. But I can't cry over spilled Kool-Aid, I have to be the best father I can be.

Steven "Chris" Ware

I looked up and the lady at the other end of the bar was still smiling in my direction. I smiled back when I realized she reminded me of my first girlfriend, Nicole.

Hell, Nicole was my first everything. I remember it like it was yesterday. I was 15 years old, and I saw her one day when I was walking home from the bus stop. She was struggling with her baby and some grocery bags. I lived in a middle-class neighborhood in the Southwest part of Little Rock off 65th street on Allison Circle. About two blocks up from my house on Butler Road were some run-down apartments. That's where Nicole was headed.

Her baby was on her hip in one arm and in the other hand she had about 3 grocery bags. I walked over to offer her some help. She looked me up and down, rolled her eyes and kept pushing. I sped up so I could get in front of her and stopped.

"Move nigga I don't have time for these games, I got shit to do," she said.

"It's obvious you need help so why you frontin?"

"You could be trying to get back to my place and rape me."

"Damn, I look like a rapist? Do I look like the type of person who rapes women, and would do it in front of their kid?"

Again, she rolled her eyes and tried to step around me. I reached in my wallet, pulled out my I.D. and said, "Look this is my I.D., if I beat you down, rape you, and kidnap your son, you'll know where to find me. So hand me the bags and let me help you."

She kept staring at my face, watching my eyes as if she was trying to get a good read on me, then she slowly handed me the bags. When her hand was free, she switched the baby to the other hip and snatched the I.D. out of my hand and kept walking. We walked in silence for a minute and then I said, "You have some pretty

brown eyes when they aren't rolling all over the place."
She didn't say a word. So I didn't say anything else.

We got to her apartment and it was amazing how clean it was. Judging from the outside of the building you would assume the inside would look just as bad. I sat the bags on the kitchen table and headed for the door. When the door was half open she stopped me. She looked like she wanted to say something but she didn't know what to say.

Finally, she spoke, "I'm sorry I was rude, you know how crazy some guys can be in these projects, but thank you. I'm getting ready to cook and if you want to, come back at about 6 or 7."

"I'll think about it," I said as I opened the door all the way.

"Jason, thanks again for the help."

"How do you know my name?"

She handed me my I.D. "It's on this, Dummy," she said with half a smile, "and that's an ugly picture. You look better in person."

"Thank you. I think."

"So are you coming back tonight or not? I'm not going to poison you."

"I'll check my schedule, I may be able to make it back." I headed home with a smile on my face. I was definitely coming back. I just didn't wanna seem too anxious.

There was a Boys and Girls Club on Harrow Road a few blocks from my house. I was there most evenings playing ball so that's where I told my parents I was gonna be. But instead I was knocking on Nicole's apartment door about 7:15.

She opened the door in a hurry, said what's up and ran back into the kitchen. R. Kelly was singing about a slow dance on her stereo. Her baby boy was fast asleep in his playpen. I looked around the living room before I sat down. She had pictures of her and her son everywhere.

I didn't see any pictures of anyone older who could have been her parents. Some of the pictures did have a guy holding the baby. He was some thugged-out looking brotha with a doo rag on his head. It made me think about how I never wore my doo rag out in public. I think that is so tacky. The waves in my hair are so tight you could use a surfboard up there. But I have never worn my head rag out of the house.

As I was walking around her living room looking at her life through her pictures, I could see her out of the corner of my eye. She was wearing some cut-off jeans and a red halter-top. She was stirring a pitcher of red Kool Aid and I was standing there staring at her.

Being so young at that time, I didn't know much about women's bodies but I was thinking hers had to be a perfect ten. She had beautiful caramel brown skin and a strong resemblance to the actress Nia Long. Her shoulder length hair was pressed straight and jet-black. I have never been a fan of color in women's hair, I always preferred it to be black.

I guess she felt me undressing her with my eyes, because she looked up and said, "Boo. I hope you like what you see."

"I think I would like it better if I had a name to go with that pretty face."

"Well Jason, my name is Nicole. Nicole Denise Dade."

"How old are you?"

"Well *you* must be young or you would know that you shouldn't ask a woman her age."

"No I didn't know that. What else I need to know?"

"Class is not in session yet. I may have to teach you a thing or two after we eat. You can go wash your hands."

When I came back, on the table was a plate of fried chicken wings, macaroni and cheese, green beans and two dinner rolls and a tall glass Kool-Aid. Everything looked good, I was impressed. She told me to go ahead and eat because the baby was up and she had to feed him.

So I sat down in the kitchen alone and ate my food. When I finished I put my plate in the sink, poured me another glass of that red deliciousness and joined her on the couch. I took a coaster off the little rack and placed my glass on the end table beside the couch.

"It's good to know you have some manners."

"You already knew that sweetheart, I did help you out earlier today."

"You did, didn't you? Thanks again for helping me, a sista was struggling trying to get to the house. So Mr. Jason, how old are *you*?"

"Well I'm 15. So I guess it's cool for you to ask me how old I am?"

"Women can ask men anything, but men have to abide by certain rules. Like men can't ask us about our age or our weight. But you're only 15?"

"Yeah, I had a big growth spurt this past summer. I'm 6 foot tall now. But again, you have me at a disadvantage because you know my age and I don't know yours."

"Well if you must know, I'm 19. I'll be 20 next month."

We sat there and talked for an hour or two. We laughed and chatted about music, movies, and relationships in general, but nothing too personal. I was learning a lot from what she said. I had only had one girlfriend up until that point. It was obvious that she had done her fair share of dating.

I watched her the whole time we talked. I couldn't take my eyes off of her. Every now and then she would look at me and smile while she talked. She seemed to really enjoy having some company to talk to. Her conversation was very animated too. Her eyes were rolling, neck was moving, and hands and arms were swinging. I just sat there like a little kid and soaked it all in.

Then her phone rang.

The smile on her face disappeared right after she said hello. She got up from the couch with the phone and went to sit at the kitchen table with her back to me. But I was still listening hard. I'm just as nosy as the next person. I heard her say Brandon was asleep in his playpen. That was a lie, he was in the playpen but he wasn't asleep. He was playing quietly. He was a good baby. The whole time I had been there he never cried. He would let out a happy scream or two while playing with his toys. But other than that, he was pretty quiet.

Then Nicole said she didn't feel like having any company. After that all I heard was a series of "no's" and "whatever nigga". After a few more minutes of that, she slammed the phone down and came back to the couch. Before she could sit down the phone rang again. She stood there looking in the direction of the phone, and then plopped down right next to me. We were closer than we were the first time. I looked at her and that same frown she had when I met her on the street was on her face.

"Nicole," I said, trying to clear the air.

"What?" She snapped back at me.

"Damn, calm down. All I want to say is, I don't need to know who that was on the phone but I would like to know what they said to you."

"Why would you wanna know that?"

"Because whatever was said to put that ugly frown on your face, I want to make sure I don't repeat it. Your face is too pretty for you to mess it up with that frown."

"That was sweet. Your innocence is adorable."

She kissed me on the cheek. Our eyes were locked to each other, as I leaned over and kissed her on the lips. After our lips touched, her tongue slowly eased into my mouth. I pulled her over on top of me so she could straddle me in my lap. Her passionate kisses made my whole body feel warm on the inside. She pulled away and rested her forehead on mine. She looked in my eyes and asked where had I learned to kiss like that. I didn't really know how to kiss I was just following her lead. And that's what I told her. Then she looked puzzled, and asked me was I a virgin. I guess the blank look on my face told her my answer was yes. She climbed off my lap and didn't say a word. She got up and put a blanket over Brandon, who had again fallen asleep. I was embarrassed. I didn't know what she was thinking.

She came back to the couch, stood over me and reached her hand out for me to stand up. She led me by the hand to her bedroom. Her bed took up most of the room. It made my twin size at home look like a cot. She told me to turn off the light and sit on the bed. I can't lie, I was so scared.

My emotions were going crazy, but she seemed to be so calm. She walked to her nightstand and turned on the lamp. When she hit the switch a red light popped on. The shit was wild, because the little boy in my pants was now a grown man and she hadn't even touched me. Next she pressed play on the radio, and Sade was singing about it not being an ordinary love. She started undressing, and while she was taking her clothes off, she was looking directly into my eyes and started talking.

"I know some women like for men to undress them, but most men are really turned on when they watch a woman take her clothes off."

She was right. I was so turned on watching her, I thought my man was going to throw up the creamy white stuff in my underwear. I had had a wet dream before but I was hoping it wouldn't happen while I was awake.

After all her clothes were off, she climbed in the bed, pushing me on my back. She was kissing me and undressing me at the same time. All the while she was still talking. Her soft voice was saying that there was something special about me. She said she was going to turn me into the perfect lover.

When all my clothes were off, she started kissing me all over my chest and was working her way down. She got to my man and put him in her mouth. I think I passed out for a few seconds, because when I felt her mouth on me, a feeling shot through my body that was unexplainable. My hands were clinching sheets, my toes were curling and my mouth was wide open. I wanted to scream. Nothing was coming out but crazy sounds. I felt like a fool. I knew she had to be holding in a laugh or something. I felt the volcano about to erupt. I tried to say something but again nothing came out.

Somehow, she knew because she stopped and was stroking my man with her hand. I exploded like a water balloon with a hole in it. She got up from the bed and told me not to move. Hell, she didn't have to worry because I was paralyzed from the neck down. The feeling that had just shot through my body had me feeling helpless. Nicole came back in the room and started wiping me off with a warm towel. When she finished she lay back on the bed and encouraged me to get on top of her.

We started kissing again. Every time she slid her sweet tasting tongue in my mouth, shock waves shot through my body. I moved down to suck on her neck. Nicole let out a few moans and quietly said, "Softer." So I did it softer, and her moans became more intense. As I gently sucked her neck, her hand started caressing her breasts.

So I moved a little further down and started kissing her right nipple. I rubbed on the left one with my thumb. After about a minute, she told me that her other nipple was getting jealous. So I started sucking the other one, then I gently pushed the two together so I could have both nipples in my mouth at the same time.

Her hands were caressing my ears, as I moved down her stomach toward her mid-section. I licked in and around her belly button. Now her hands were rubbing the top of my head as she moaned and wiggled around on her back like she had to pee. She started pushing me downtown. Hell, I had never been uptown, so you know I knew nothing about going downtown. The only downtown shopping I knew about is what I saw watching Vanessa Del Rio porn videos.

I sat up a little bit when she spread her legs wider. She put both hands down there and spread her lips. She touched the little third nipple and said, "Kiss me right here."

So I did.

I kissed the third nipple over and over. Then I started sucking it. She asked me to stop. She told me to give her my hand. She started kissing and sucking my index finger. Her kisses were soft. Her tongue glided across my finger slow and easy.

"That's how you do it," she said.

So I started up again. This time I did it the way she showed me, slow and easy. My face was buried between her legs. I slid my tongue inside her while her hands went back and forth from my head to her breasts. Her squirming and moaning really turned me on. Then all of a sudden, her legs closed on my head. Her body was shaking like a butt-naked crackhead in the snow. Her breathing was real heavy and then she kinda exhaled.

She pulled me up to her face and kissed me intensely. Her hands were searching for and found my little soldier. He was standing up at full attention. She placed him inside of her. I can't begin to explain how it felt. The grind was slow as we kissed each other. Her fingernails were stroking my back. After about 30 minutes the volcano erupted again. This time I exploded inside her. I rolled off her and stared up at the ceiling. She put her arm around me and buried her head in my chest. Her leg was on top of mine, and again she started caressing my ear. I looked over at her alarm clock and it read 2:37.

I got up and put on my pants. She sat up and told me to sit back down for a second. I did. She came up from behind and put her hand on my shoulder and started talking in my ear.

"J, whenever you make love to a woman you do it just like we did. Listen to her, do what she likes. It doesn't take much to please a man in bed, but sometimes it takes a lot more patience to please a woman. I've been hurt a lot, but there is something about you that just feels right. I think you can make me happy again. Take care of me and I'll take care of you."

She kissed my cheek and laid back down. I didn't say anything, I didn't know what to say. I just kept getting dressed. When I finished, I leaned over and kissed her on the lips and told her I would see her tomorrow.

I walked home with a smile on my face. Those last words she spoke replayed over and over in my head. "Something about you just feels right." I told myself at that moment that I would not disappoint her. I would try like hell to make her happy.

The next day when I got off the bus, I went straight to her house to get her phone number because the grits hit the fan after that night. I was locked down like Alcatraz for coming home so late. Like Forrest Gump said, Nicole and I were like peas and carrots from that day forward.

Damn.

Nicole Denise Dade, I haven't thought of her in a long time.

DeShon

Tragedy

M e and the boys hit the Matrix about 12:30. Reggie and Johnny hit the dance floor as soon as we walked in. I headed for the bar to look for Jason. I was already good and tipsy. I had been sipping on some gin already. You know how we do, we got to get drunk before we get to the club. No one wants to spend all their money on those high priced, watered down drinks. I bought a Corona at the overly crowded bar to keep my buzz as I walked around the club to look for Jason.

The four us been tight like brothers since high school. We were basketball stars at McClellan and have been running the streets together ever since. We all were out celebrating our new freedom. Jason finalized his divorce earlier today and Erica had fired me a couple of weeks ago. For a minute, I thought she was the one but I guess her and that other dude thought otherwise. Yeah I got played, but it's cool she'll need me before I need her. I spotted Jason and walked over to his table.

"Man, I started to act like I don't know you. Dude you sitting here looking pretty homely. Man, get up and dance with somebody. Looks like you up in here daydreaming. Don't be up in here pouting."

"Yeah D, I'm cool man, how you doing?"

I smiled, "I'm sorry J, how you doing bro? But for real, I'm just saying we can't have you sitting here looking sour running off the ladies. What's on your mind?"

"Man, please, you should want me to run 'em off, it's a hoodrat convention in here tonight. Where's Reggie and Johnny?"

"Look at the dance floor."

"That's messed up. They could have come and showed they boy some love before they get their freak-on."

"Well I did, now I'm gonna hit the dance floor. You coming?"

"I guess but I got dibs on the sista in the jean skirt."

"Damn she fine, go head do your thing. I'll find somebody else."

I was never really a club person but every time I went I had a pretty good time. The liquor had a lot to do with that because it gave me that edge. I knew I couldn't find a good woman in here. Most of these chicks were weaved up with their Citi Trends outfits on. So I was just going to dance a little, drink a lot and try to take my mind off of Erica.

Most of the ladies in the house ran to the floor when the DJ played the "Wobble." After that he played "Back that Azz Up" to get the fellas up. I tried to find the biggest booty in the house. When I found her she was bouncing and shaking it like she was auditioning for a twerk video.

Johnny was dancing with a big girl. He was about 6'5" and 270lbs, but he was all muscle, a dark brown brick wall. The girl he was dancing with had to be about 250 herself. He likes 'em big.

Reggie was dancing with a petite chick with long spiral curls. She had a real pretty face but she was a bit too thin for my taste.

Denim skirt was still all up on my man J, and I was glad his mind didn't seem to be on his divorce. He deserves a good time.

The girl in front of me was actually pretty cute. Plus, she had enough backside to make a lot of brothas weak at the knees. She was probably a lifetime member at this joint. Then I got this feeling someone was watching me. I looked up and straight ahead was a pretty little face staring at mine. She was sitting at a table with her girls drinking what looked to be a Sex on the Beach. The girl I was dancing with turned around and put her arms around my neck and was saying something.

"What did you say?"

"I said you're kinda cute. What's your name? I'm Keisha."

"Oh, my name is DeShon."

I gave her a fake smile and looked up to see if the mystery lady was still watching. Damn, she was gone. The whole table was empty. I took a quick glance around the club. She was nowhere to be found. Double damn. Petey Pablo had the club patrons spinning their shirts like helicopters. Keisha still had her arms around my neck and had a big smile on her face like she had just exhaled and I was her man. "Hot in Here" by Nelly started blasting through the speakers. Keisha turned around again and started shaking what her mamma gave her.

Someone bumped into me from behind. I looked to see who it was and it was the girl from the table. She said excuse me and winked. I had to get Keisha the hell away from me. I saw Reggie doing his thang with some bucktooth sistah. He needed saving worse than me. He made eye contact with me and I gave him a head nod. He knew what was up. Reg turned and started dancing with Keisha. I grabbed Bugs Bunny before she could get mad at Reg. I got behind her and gave the head nod to the brother with the jheri curl standing on the side of the dance floor. He eagerly walked up and started dancing with Bugs. I disappeared like David Copperfield.

Just when I looked to find the mystery lady a slow record came on. It was "Nobody" by Keith Sweat. She found me and grabbed my hand. We started a slow grind that had my nature rising fast. I knew she could feel me poking her so I backed up a little. She pulled me closer. She looked up at me to give me a sexy little smile and bit her lip. We were making love on the dance floor. She let go and led me by the hand off the dance floor before the song was over. We went right past the bar and out the front door.

"Did you drive?" She asked.

"Yeah, I'm parked out there."

This girl was so sexy and her hand felt so soft. She was wearing an orange shirt that was cut short at the stomach. Her belly ring was shining. The low rider pants she had on showed off her thong panties. It's something about those thongs that drive most brothas crazy. My straight jacket was already on and I was ready for them to take me to the padded room. After we got to my truck I hit the unlock button on my key ring and reached for the door.

"No. Let's stand out here and talk. I just wanted to lean on something while I try to give you a little PDA."

"How you know I like people leaning up against my shit?"

She smiled and said, "Well I didn't know you were a balla pushing a Denali. Are you the Nino Brown of Little Rock?"

"No darling, I'm not a street pharmacist. I work hard to buy nice things. So basically you thought I was driving a hoopty."

I was up against the driver's side door. She walked up in my space.

"It didn't matter if you were in a hooptie or a Hummer, my mind was made up when you walked through the door."

I smiled, "So you have been stalking me all night?"

"You can call it what you want Mr. Bryson, I know a good man when I see one."

"So you know my name already?"

"Yes I do, DeShon Bryson. I'm Crystal Thomas. I asked one of your friends about you at the bar. He told me your name and that you had just broke up with your girlfriend. I think he said her name was Erica."

She had to be talking about Johnny. He is the only one who would have been at the bar giving up that kind of info.

"Well remind me to slap him later for telling you all my business."

"I don't know all of your info, yet."

"What else do you need to know?"

"Well the only other thing I want to know is, do you want me as much as I want you?"

Before I could say another word, she kissed me. It was a soft, simple kiss, a kiss someone gives you when you have done something nice for them. She pulled me closer and kissed me again. This time, she slid her tongue in my mouth. This was a long sexy kiss. She pulled away, bit her lip and smiled.

"You look so sexy when you bite your lip like that."

"Thank you. You make me feel sexy looking at me with those seductive eyes."

"I know, bedroom eyes, it's my curse."

"A curse? I would think you would want eyes that turn women on."

"Well it's cool sometimes but with these eyes women can usually tell what I'm thinking."

"Well if you're thinking what I'm thinking, let's go to your place. Do you live alone?"

"Yes Ma'am."

"Let's go."

"Now?"

"Well after I tell my girls I'm leaving. You can take me to my friend's house to get my car and I'll trail you to your spot."

"Sounds like a plan."

We went back into the club. Reggie was standing near the dance floor talking to a pretty girl with an ugly weave. I walked up to him to tell him that I was leaving.

"Excuse me sweetheart, I need to holla at my homeboy real quick."

She rolled her eyes at me, smiled at Reggie and walked off.

"Thanks for saving me man. I've heard of wet and wavy but why wear a weave that's dry and nappy."

"Tell Jason to give you and Johnny a ride home. I'm leaving."

"Why man? It's women everywhere. Fuck Erica. Grab one of these ladies and have a good time."

Crystal walked up, grabbed my hand and told me she was ready. Reggie started smiling and gave me a pound. They said their hellos and goodbye's all in the same sentence.

Her friend's house was close, right off 36th street just a few blocks from the club. On the way, she flipped through my CD's. She wanted to hear New Edition's greatest hits. We listened to "Mr. Telephone Man" twice before we got to her car. She drove a midnight blue Toyota Camry.

My apartment was on the other side of town right off Cantrell Road. I was still under the influence so I really needed to get off of these streets. When we got to my place it was about 1:30 am. I knew my house was clean but I was worried about the bathroom. Both my dogs had done the three S's at my place before we left for the club. I knew them niggas left the bathroom fucked up. So I would have to clean it up but if she really had to go she could use the one in my bedroom.

We walked in and I told her to make herself at home. I headed straight for the bathroom. When I came out she was at my bookcase looking at the books and pictures.

"Is this your daughter?" She asked.

"No, that's my goddaughter Niya."

"She is so precious. How old is she?"

"She will be six in February."

"You read all these?"

"Yes ma'am. I did."

"Oh really!"

"You don't believe me?"

"Which one of these Eric Jerome Dickey books did you like the most?"

"Liar's Game is one of the best by far."

"What was the main character's name?"

"Vince and his girl's name was Dana. Any more pop quiz questions, Professor Thomas?"

She smiled, "That's all for now. You have a really nice place."

"Damn, you say that like you're surprised."

"I'm not surprised. I'm impressed. You have this place decorated better than mine. Did you do this all by yourself?"

"Actually, I picked out all of the statues, artwork and plants, but my mother put everything where it is."

"You have good taste. Are all the paintings by the same person?"

"Ninety percent of them. Most are by an artist named Kevin A. Williams. Let me show you the ones in the bedroom."

She smiled and bit her lip again. "You think you're slick, but it's cool, trying to lure me to your den of sin."

"It's not like that, it's just that the ones in the room are R-rated."

"Yeah right!"

"I have bedroom eyes remember. It won't take much to lure you to my bed."

"Touché'! After you."

"No ma'am, after you." I let her go in first.

"This one is called *Light My Fire*, and the other one is *Right Now*.

"Whoa, R-rated, these are more like NC-17. They're nice though. DeShon, is this Erica?"

Damn, I had pictures of me and Erica all over my mirror.

"Yeah, that's her."

"She's pretty. What did you do to her?"

"Why do you assume it's my fault?"

"It's always the man's fault one way or another."

"Not this time my darling, she had another man. That's why we broke up."

She walked up to me and kissed me on the lips and grabbed me between the legs.

"Why did she need another man? Weren't you man enough for her?"

"I guess not, I . . ."

"Take your clothes off."

"Excuse me?"

"You heard me, take your clothes off."

She sat down on my bed, kicked her shoes off and crossed her legs. I paused for a second, said what the hell and started to unbutton my shirt. I did it slowly while she stared at me. I placed the shirt on top of the hamper near the dresser and started taking off my shoes and pants. Now I'm standing in front of her in my t-shirt and boxers.

"I know you're not done. I want all your clothes off. You got naked bodies all over the wall so you can't be shy."

"No shame in my game."

I pulled my t-shirt over my head then kicked my boxers off. My little soldier was standing at full attention. He was waiting patiently for the sexy lady drill sergeant to give him his orders. She pulled me toward her and took me in her mouth. I damn near fell on top of her when my knees got weak. I was about to lose control. I tried to pull back but she put her hands on my hips and pulled me back toward her. After a few minutes, I exploded in her mouth and I almost felt lightheaded.

She stood and I reached for her shirt but she stopped me. She turned me around and pushed me back on the bed. She bit her lip and started undressing. Her eyes were on mine and my eyes were all over her. Her light brown body was flawless. She came to the bed and straddled me. I started kissing and sucking her neck. My hands were gently moving up and down her back. She pushed me down on my back. That's twice now that she played the aggressive role. She was confident about what she wanted and what she wanted to do. I liked it. It was turning me on even more. She sat up and started caressing my chest. She dug her fingernails deep in my chest then down to my abs.

"Do you have protection?"

"Right here!"

"Damn, Mr. Boy Scout, always prepared huh?"

"Yeah, it's been in my hand since I took off my pants."

"Good, I thought that was a hang nail scratching me on my back."

We both laughed. I opened the package and put it on. This thin layer of latex has stopped many long-tailed army men from invading the gates of the egg empire. I climbed on top of her and slipped my key into her door. I unlocked all her moans and groans as I slid in and out. Her nails were piercing the skin on my back as the grind got faster. Her moaning intensified and she grabbed me tighter and bit down on my collarbone. Her leg was shaking and my body was aching from her teeth in my flesh. Her heavy breathing slowed down and she loosened her grip.

She told me to sit up at the end of the bed. So I did. I was the slave. She was the master. She got up and sat down on my key of love but she had her back to me. Crystal knew how to please a man. A least she knew how to please this man. She put her hands on my knees and treated me like I was Ginuwine and rode my pony. After only a few minutes, I felt the volcano about to erupt. The latex shield kept all of the hot lava from sliding down the mountain to attack the egg people. I got up and went to the bathroom, tied a knot in the condom and flushed it down the toilet. When I came out, she was standing in the mirror wearing the shirt I had just taken off.

I walked up and put my arms around her.

"What's on your mind?" I asked.

"Nothing really, how tall are you? This shirt fits me like a dress."

"I'm six feet three inches."

She smiled, "You're my 6'3", almond brown Mandingo."

"Almond brown? I see you're a Martin Lawrence fan."

"Yep, I have his show on DVD. I guess we look like an alright couple."

"Only alright?"

"Well, you and her look real cute together. You look happy with her."

"I was but I guess the other guy made her happier."

"You still have feelings for her, don't you?"

"Of course, I can't turn my emotions on and off like a lamp. I just have to replace thoughts of her with thoughts of someone else, someone like you."

"An honest man, where have you been hiding?"

"Hiding behind dead end relationships I guess."

She turned to face me and buried her head in my chest. I felt warm tears falling on my cold skin. I led her back to the bed so we could lie down. She wrapped her arm tightly around me and kept her head in my chest. I gently ran my fingers through her hair and kissed her on the top of her head.

"I'm sorry I spoiled the mood."

"It's cool. Is there something you want to talk about?"

"Not really. I'll be okay. If you don't mind me asking, what do the initials on your chest stand for?"

"Well, the girl I was with before Erica had a miscarriage. We had already picked out names, Kasi Janee if it were a girl, and DeShon Jerrell if it were a boy. I had their initials tattooed on my chest about a month later."

"I'm sorry to hear that. What happened with you and her?"

"We just grew apart. Tragedy usually makes relationships stronger or helps destroy them, it destroyed ours."

"You know what DeShon, I'm starting to really like you."

I smiled. "I'm starting to like you too."

Jason

How'd You Get My Number

After dropping off those two knuckleheads, it was 5a.m when I got home. I jumped in the shower. As the hot water ran down my body, my thoughts were on my night out. I actually had a good time. Johnny and Reggie had me cracking up talking about the women in the club. All the rainbow weaves and skank outfits can make an entertaining night. I danced with a girl named Kim most of the night, she seemed cool. The jean skirt and silk blouse really looked nice on her. Her skin was soft and she smelled so sweet. I was kinda nervous, it was the first woman I had been close to other than Monica in about five years.

Three years of dating and two years of marriage, all with the same woman, had me feeling awkward when Kim was slow grinding on me. But her looking and smelling good made me feel a lot better. She was playing me real close, but not as close as the chick DeShon left with.

I turned the water off and stepped out of the shower in front of the mirror. I wiped the steam off to look at myself. My hair and beard were trimmed nice. At 24 years old, I was in my prime. My wardrobe is up to date, so I hope getting back in the dating game won't be too hard on me.

I pulled back the covers to lay down, and before my head hit the pillow, my mind was back on my time dating Nicole.

Back then Sunday evening was our movie night. Basketball kept me busy most of the week. The games were on Tuesdays and Fridays, and we practiced after school the other days. Plus, Nicole stayed busy during the week herself. She was always reading or studying. So we only saw each other on the weekends. She would come to the game on Fridays and we would be together all day Saturday and Sunday. On Saturdays we would take her son Brandon to the park or push him around the mall in his stroller.

I was a junior, and I was the shit at the school.

As the starting point guard on the team, I was averaging 17 points, 11 assists, 6 rebounds, and 2 steals per game. Yeah, I had game, but my game is not what gave me my superstar status at the school.

Well it helped my rep, but everyone was on my jock because of Nicole. All the guys were a bit jealous because I had a girl that was twenty years old. And all the females were standing in line for me because they wanted to know what a 20-year-old woman wanted with a 16-year-old boy.

I didn't consider myself a boy. I was far from a man but I was more mature than a little boy. Reggie had told the whole team Nicole and I were having sex. So all the girls were really curious to see what I had to offer. Some of the girls at the school were fine and if the circumstances were different, I would have hooked up with one of them. But I was dedicated to Nicole, she had taught me a lot about love and life. She would always tell me that if we ever broke up my next girlfriend would be spoiled rotten. "She wouldn't know how to act with a man like you," is what she would say.

Nicole taught me the simple things that I could do to make most women feel good. For example she told me most women like to feel loved and appreciated, whether it be in words or deeds. Nicole liked for me to call her "my Boo" or "my Shorty". She would tell me, "Some women don't like that kind of stuff. It is a man's job to find out the things his woman likes. He is supposed to do these things without hesitation."

Whenever it was time for me to leave, I would say, "Ok Boo, it's time for me to go." Then I would get up from the couch and reach out my hand to her so that she could pull herself up. She would poke out her bottom lip like a little kid who was sad because they couldn't get what they wanted. We would hold hands as we walked to the door. Then I would turn around, wrap my arms around her waist and give her a big hug. Since I was a few inches taller she had to tiptoe to kiss me good night. Sometimes after that kiss, I would look into her beautiful brown eyes and I would be in her bedroom another few hours. Then I would finally leave, walking home on cloud nine.

Steven "Chris" Ware
63

I remember the night we played North Little Rock High School. We were ranked #2 in the state, they were #3. They were a team that always had talent but they lacked discipline. We were expected to win but it would be an all-out war. DeShon was our leading scorer. This kid had some serious game. DeShon and his girl Tiffany would kick it with Nicole and me from time to time. We would get together, watch movies or play cards. Tiffany ran her mouth at school about my business too, but other than that she was cool. Nicole and Brandon, Tiffany, and my parents sat together at the games. My folks were okay with Nicole. Nicole and basketball kept me out of trouble. If I wasn't with Nicole I was at practice.

It was game time. We were already on the floor. Before the jump ball I looked into the eyes of my teammates. In their eyes I saw no fear. DeShon, Johnny, Reggie and Pat all had the eye of the tiger. To calm my nerves, I would look up in the stands at Nicole to wink at her. I pounded on my chest three times and I was ready. We won the jump ball when Pat tapped the ball over to me. The guy guarding me was only about 5'6". I called a play so that everyone would clear the lane so that I could take him off the dribble. I hit him with a Tim Hardaway killa crossover. He stole the ball and took off down court. I tried to hustle back but he dropped off a pass to the man trailing. We were down 2-0. DeShon took the ball out and passed it in to me. Now this lil' bitty dude guarding me got a smirk on his face. I dribbled up past half court sizing him up. He was playing back a little bit, so when I got to the 3-point line, I pulled up. Before I could get the shot off he slapped the ball away. He slowed down to walk the ball up. He smiled and said, "Yeah nigga, I know your game. Coach had me watch your game film. It's going to be a long night."

Ok, now I'm a nigga. Nicole hated that I had that word in my vocabulary. So I had myself a trash talker and better yet he thought he knew my game. They worked the ball around and when the ball got back to Webster he shot a three. Swish, we were down 5-0. I took the inbound pass and pushed the ball up the court. I called play three and dished the ball to DeShon. Everyone else cleared the lane and I went down low and posted up on

"Mini Me". DeShon passed the ball back in to me when I was set. I spun around and laid it off the glass with ease. He can't handle my 6'3" frame. They worked the ball down court and passed it down low to their big man. He made his move like he was playing in slow motion. He tried to shoot the ball but Johnny blocked it. I picked up the loose ball and walked it up the court. I called play three again. Everybody got in position, and again, I went to the post and caught the pass from DeShon.

This time the defense closed in and DeShon took off toward the basket. I hit him with the give and go. He got the ball, took a flight that ended with a rim rocking two-handed dunk. We both chest bumped and hollered at the top of our lungs right under the basket, just like Larry Johnson used to do when he was at the top of his game with the Charlotte Hornets. We went on a 10-2 run, and at the end of the first quarter we were up 25-11. We ended up winning 87-52. DeShon scored 26 points and had 15 rebounds. I had 15 points and 11 assists.

After the games Nicole waited for me to shower, and we rode home with my folks.

My senior year started great with only a few changes. We entered the basketball season ranked #1 in the state. Little Rock Parkview won the state championship the previous year. Our team, who lost in the semi-finals, had all our starters back. Again, I was the big dawg on campus. Everything with Nicole was cool except for the fact that Brandon's daddy John, started coming around.

Brandon needed to know his father, but he was always abusive with Nicole. He wasn't really a thug. He was just an intelligent fool from the projects with a temper problem. He went to the University of Central Arkansas on a scholarship. He was on academic probation so he sat out a semester. Nicole said John's daddy used to beat up his mother and she believed that's why John was messed up in the head. Nicole said he had only been around Brandon a few times. Nicole and I had been together almost two years and he hadn't seen Brandon once until recently.

DeShon and I had decided to go to school here in the city at the University of Arkansas at Little Rock (UALR). We took time and weighed options of what the other schools had to offer. UALR was the best fit for both of us. DeShon had dreams of playing in the NBA. I did too, but I wasn't dead set on it like he was. I really just wanted to make sure my education would be paid for. We kept it secret and promised not to tell anyone until the time was right. I just hoped I could make it to graduation without any drama.

One Saturday afternoon I was at Nicole's place asleep in her bedroom. I woke up when I heard a heated conversation going on in the front room. It was John and Nicole arguing. I didn't want to make the situation worse so I stayed in the back and listened close.

"So what's this I hear, you fucking some young cat now?"

"That's none of your damn business. The only thing you need to be worried about in this house is this little boy right here."

"That's what I'm worried about. I don't want you tricking and having all kinds of men around my son, especially little young boys."

"Hearing you say some dumb shit like that to me lets me know Jason is more of a man than you will ever be. I can't believe you just stood there and called me a hoe. You know me better than that."

My blood was boiling. I wanted to go out there and check this fool but I kept my cool. I knew Nicole could handle herself. I just didn't like his tone or the way he was talking about her and me. They argued for about twenty more minutes then I heard something that sounded like a slap and something hitting the floor. Then I heard Brandon screaming. I ran in the room and Brandon was standing over his mother, who was on the floor holding her face. I lost it. Before I knew it, I was in John's ass. I beat his ass like I was Forrest protecting his precious Jenny.

Nicole finally pulled me off of him.

"Nigga don't you ever put your hands on her again! What kind of shit is that? How you gon' hit her in front of your son?"

"Jason be cool, I'm alright."

"Naw, fuck that. Look at your face. It's already swelling up. Let me finish handling this nigga for you. Show him how us 'young cats' like to get down."

"Jason please, watch your mouth. Just take Brandon to the back. I'll be fine."

Brandon, who was still whimpering, was holding on to Nicole's leg. He was staring dead at John. If John had taken a step toward Nicole I believe he would have tried to attack John himself. I looked at John. I looked into his eyes, I could see his fear. I picked up Brandon who was reluctant to leave his mother's side. I told him it was okay and took him to the back. After a few minutes I heard the door slam. Nicole came in the room and grabbed her son. She held him close to her as tears rolled down her face. I didn't know what to say. I sat down on the bed beside her and put my arm around her. She put her head on my shoulder.

"Jason you know I hate it when you use that type of language, especially the "N" word."

Nothing else was said, and we just sat there thinking our own thoughts.

Weeks went by and she didn't hear from John. I guess everything was back to normal. Basketball season had started and we were 8-0 leading up to the Parkview game. It was the first conference game for both of us. They had been upset by Pine Bluff high school, but they still were ranked #2. So this Friday night the Lions Den, our home floor, would be packed.

My senior year was blowing by like a tornado. I had already ordered my cap and gown, and everybody was excited about the prom. A girl name Shuntae Radford had asked me to take her to the prom. She knew I had a girl but she joked and said maybe that old lady I was going with didn't want to hang out with a bunch of high school kids all night. Shuntae was real cool. We had a few classes together. She had to be one of the finest young ladies to ever walk the halls of McClellan. She had a fair skin complexion and a smile that made all the fellas pause when she walked into the room. It was obvious she was interested in me. I could see it in her eyes every time we spoke. We would chitchat at lunch and after school from time to time. She was on the drill team and was the football homecoming Queen. If I weren't with Nicole, I probably would have been with Shuntae. The beautiful Ms. Radford would have been on my arm on prom night. But actually, Nicole was excited about going to the prom because she didn't get to go to hers. It was only January, and the prom wasn't until late April. She talked about it all the time and she had already picked out her dress. All I had on my mind was the game on Friday.

Wednesday before the big game, Nicole called when I got home from practice, and told me we needed to talk. So I grabbed my coat and headed to her apartment. I walked in and gave her a big hug and kiss. I had not seen her since Sunday. I sensed something was up. I always could tell people's emotions through their eyes, especially hers. I could tell she was getting ready to talk about something serious. She was standing at the window closest to the door. I walked up behind her and started massaging her shoulders.

"What's on your mind Boo?"

She sighed and said, "I hate to say this, but me and John are getting back together."

I thought she was joking so I smiled and said, "If you hate to say it, why say it at all?"

She turned to face me and when I looked in her eyes I knew she wasn't joking. I just stood there, speechless. She kept talking but I really wasn't listening. She told me he called and apologized Sunday after I left. Not just about what had happened a few weeks ago but about everything. He apologized for not being there for his son. He told her the ass whipping he took from that young dude made him do a lot of thinking. She went on and on about how he said he needed to change his life for his son's sake. It all sounded fake to me. He didn't give a damn about Brandon. He just didn't like the fact that Nicole seemed happy with someone other than him. I couldn't believe what I was hearing.

"Nicole, you really believe all of this. Everything you just told me he has said before. So what's so different now?"

"He seems sincere this time. Brandon needs to know who his father is."

"I can understand that, but ya'll don't have to be a couple for him to be a man and take care of his child."

"Jason please, you're making this harder than it needs to be."

"What kind of nonsense is that? This is hard for me. You know how I feel about you. I love you."

She sighed, pulled away from me and faced the window. Her silence hurt me. "How could you do this to me? All the time I spent with you and Brandon meant nothing?"

More silence, she didn't even turn around. I moved up closer to her and put my hand on her shoulder. "Have you really thought about this? I mean this dude continues to hurt you every time he comes around."

"Brandon needs his father and that's all I have to say."

"Nicole, do you love me?" More silence. "Have you ever loved me?"

She turned around and looked at me. I looked at her eyes. I couldn't read her thoughts because of her tears.

"I think it's time for you to go."

"Nicole, wait." I said, reaching for her hand.

She took a step back from me, "No Jason, just go."

I stood there for a second. I left when she turned and went back to the window. The rest of the night and all day Thursday I was a zombie. I was completely out of it. I couldn't believe it was over just like that. I know I was being a bit selfish. I think I hurt her when I questioned her about loving me. I knew she loved me. Brandon did need to be around his father, but I had love for the little guy too. I just couldn't understand why I couldn't be in the picture. I guess this was bigger than me. I had to get my act together before the game. This was the biggest game of my life and I had to be ready.

The Lion's Den was filled to capacity. I tried to block thoughts of Nicole out of my mind. I was feeling pretty good until I saw her walk in. Only this time she was sitting on the visitor's side. I still was cool. But right before the ref threw up the jump ball, I glanced at Nicole as usual, to wink. That was such a natural part of my pre-game routine that I had looked her way without thinking. That's when I saw John walk in with some popcorn and a drink and sit beside Nicole. She saw me watching and put her head down. He saw me too and immediately looked at her. He leaned over said something to her then glanced back at me. I looked away. My blood was hotter than lava. Something had to happen to calm my nerves. That's when I heard a voice say, "Do your thing J." I looked up and it was Shuntae on the sidelines with the drill team. She was smiling and waving at me. That's all I needed.

I pounded my fist on my chest three times, and I was ready. Parkview won the tip and their point guard started up the court. He glanced at the coach who was calling out a play. I stepped up and stole the ball. I dribbled down the court and did a reverse dunk. I swung off the rim and when I landed I pointed up into the stands where our drill team was. The crowd went wild. I looked over at Shuntae and winked at her. She looked at the girl beside her as if to say, "Girl did you see the way he looked at me?"

I got back down court. They tried to work the ball inside, but Pat stole it. He got the ball to me. DeShon and I raced back down court. I was in the middle of the floor. He was on the right wing, so I dropped him a sweet behind the back pass. He rose up with a two-hand dunk that had the whole goal shaking when he came down off the rim. Parkview called time-out. DeShon and I yelled and chest bumped each other under our basket on the way back to the bench. I looked up at John, who was still watching me.

"Yeah nigga, I got some game," I thought to myself.

By halftime Parkview had got their act together. It was toward the end of the third quarter, and we were only up by two. I only had 8 points, but I was having a hell of a game. I already had 12 assists, 8 rebounds, and 4 steals. I made a move toward the basket and got fouled. I came down hard on my ankle. When my body hit the floor, I screamed and held my ankle. Pain went from my foot and shot up my whole body. The crowd was silent. The trainer was telling me to stay calm.

After a few minutes on the floor, I got up and put my arm around the shoulders of the trainer and one of the other coaches. They carried me to the locker room. Coach Davis went back to the game and left me with the trainer, who we called Coach Belmont. I was waiting for him to wrap my ankle when my father walked in. Coach and my dad started talking.

"Coach Belmont, can we speed this up. Wrap up my ankle so I can get back out there."

"Son, Coach Belmont said that when he looked at your foot it looks more severe that an ankle sprain. It may be your achilles tendon. He can't be sure without an x-ray but you're done for the night."

"Done for the night." Those words replayed over and over in my head as I lay back on the table. I wanted to cry, but I couldn't. I was too frustrated, angry and hurt to cry. I was frustrated I couldn't get back in the game.

I was angry at Nicole for coming to the game with John and my foot was hurting like hell. One lonely tear slid down my face. Daddy helped me into the shower. I was pulling my head through my shirt when Coach Belmont came back with some crutches. I limped back to the bench to watch the rest of the game. There was only 2 minutes left and all eyes were on me. I was in street clothes so they knew I wasn't getting back in the game. We were clinging to a 3-point lead. I looked up at John and Nicole. John had a look on his face like he was happy about my foot. Nicole had a look of concern on her face. I looked around and Shuntae had the same expression as Nicole. My mind went into a trance. I was thinking about Nicole and what we had. Brandon and Nicole were part of John's family now. Who am I to keep her from being happy?

I didn't notice it at first but while my mind was wandering I was staring directly at Shuntae. Before I knew it, the horn had sounded and the crowd was going crazy. I looked up at the scoreboard and we had won 63-60. Shuntae came right to the bench and asked if I was okay.

I tried to smile and said, "I'm cool."

"I saw your girl sitting over there with another guy. So I know you're not that cool. You were over here staring into space like you have a lot on your mind. If you want to talk, call me. I'm headed home right now."

I looked up at her eyes and I saw true concern on her face.

Nicole and John were walking up the bleachers. She was looking down at Shuntae and me.

"Ok, pretty lady I'll call you, what's your number?"

"Well, I don't have a pen, but I already got your number. I'll call you about 10:30."

I smiled and asked, "How did you get my number?"

She matched my smile and replied, "Luv, I have had your number since junior high."

With the past fresh on my mind, I fell asleep with a smile on my face.

Nicole

A Lot to Deal With

I just left the gym from my son's 1st basketball game. I was waiting patiently in the car for him to come out of the locker room. Brandon was a 7th grader at Conway Middle School and I was beyond impressed. His life revolved around basketball because all his free time was spent playing at the park down the street from our house. One day when I got home from work, he begged me to buy him these Better Basketball DVD's. I knew it was a good investment because after homework and playing outside, that's about all he watches on T.V. Now after tonight, I know first-hand he has been paying attention to those DVD's.

Brandon was amazing for lack of a better word. I'm a fan of the game so I had pen and paper trying to keep up with his stats. My son ended up with 13 points, 8 assists, 5 rebounds, 2 steals, 1 block, and 2 turnovers. He started the game and played most of it without any rest. He reminds me of a mini Allen Iverson. Although I think at this point Brandon and Iverson are the same height. I'm a proud single mom whose 12-year-old son just put a Chester Cheetah smile on my face. My smile got a little wider when I saw him walk toward the car.

I couldn't hide my excitement.

"Hey Big Man! You didn't tell me you were *that* good."

He started grinning, "I didn't know either, but I do know I was nervous."

"You didn't look nervous to me. I guess those DVD's paid off."

"Yep, I love 'em and I watch Jason's old game tapes too."

"Jason's game tapes? Where did you get those?"

"They were in a box in my closet. I thought you put them in there for me."

Wow, Jason's game tapes. Jason had been my boyfriend years ago. I wanted to give him back his tapes after we broke up but I never got around to it. Our bitter break-up anniversary is coming up soon. It's been almost 10 years, and I still think about him. Hearing Brandon say his name quickly brought back so many good memories.

"Do you know who Jason is?"

"Kinda. He used to be your boyfriend, right? His face looks familiar on those tapes. He was a really good point guard, I was trying to play like him."

"Yeah, he was pretty good. He's a good player to pattern your game after, cause your daddy definitely couldn't play."

"Dang Momma, you just ruined my mood."

"How is that?"

"Bringing up my father. I don't have a daddy."

"Don't say things like that, you have a daddy. Just because he doesn't come around like he's supposed to doesn't mean he don't exist."

"He's not God momma. I'm supposed to be able to see him and touch him if he is real. Besides, if he was around it would be trouble anyway, because if I see him hit you again it's gonna get ugly."

"Before I deal with your lil smart mouth, you can remember us fighting?"

"I don't remember *you* fighting but I remember him punching you two different times. The first time I remember somebody coming in stopping it, the next time he hit you and left. We've seen him maybe twice since then."

This boy has a good memory. He had to be 5 or 6 when that happened, and it would explain why Brandon never wanted anything to do with his daddy, even when he did come around. Brandon never even mentioned his daddy. I always found that odd. I understand it now, he hates him.

"Look baby I know John hasn't been any kind of father to you. But I don't want you walking around here with resentment and hatred in your heart."

Brandon was staring out his window twirling that ball in his hands. He turned towards me and said, "You think I hate him? I'm old enough to realize you have to really know who a person is to hate who they are. I hate what I saw him do to you, other than that, I don't know nothing about that dude. And I don't really wanna know."

"Well you obviously have some strong opinions about him, so it's safe to say you have been thinking about him."

He huffed, "I hadn't thought about him in a while. If you had not brought him up I wouldn't have been thinking about him now. Only thing obvious to me is the fact he doesn't care about either of us. Do *you* think about him?"

"You know what? Your smart mouth almost got you slapped. But I'm a little more hurt that I am mad. You will not disrespect me like that. I am your momma not one of your school mates. We'll definitely finish this conversation when we get home cuz you don't need to say anything else to me right now."

I don't know who this boy thinks he's talking to but I ain't the one. We have a lot to deal with when we get home.

I pressed the gas pedal a little harder as the tears began to fall down my face.

Jason

What Goes Around Comes Around

I pulled out of the dealership feeling like a big shot. My brand new Infa-red Cadillac Escalade sitting on chrome 22" rims had me feeling like a million bucks. After the drama I've been through the past couple of months this truck was an early birthday gift to myself.

I start my new job at the university next week. I was hired as an assistant coach at my alma mater, the University of Arkansas at Little Rock (UALR). My duties would include recruiting and scouting local talent, as well as helping the point guards with their ball handling and decision making.

My playing days were never the same after I tore my Achilles in high school, but UALR still gave DeShon and me scholarships. D was a regular starter all four years and I was a top reserve player, who made my contributions off the bench. My man D was 1st team, All

Sun Belt Conference our senior year. He even had few NBA try-outs but he never signed with anyone. We both got degrees in Physical Education. He was a P.E teacher and head basketball coach at Southwest Middle School.

DeShon, Reggie, Johnny and I were 4 of the 5 starters from my high school basketball team. We lost the state championship our senior year. I was on the bench in a cast and street clothes, cheering the guys on while wishing I was on the floor.

My relationship with DeShon was a little stronger because we both grew up on Allison Circle in a middle-class neighborhood in the southwest corner of Little Rock. Johnny and Reggie were cousins. Johnny stayed a bikes-ride away on Lancaster Drive. Reggie was actually from the northside of the town. He was from a rough community called McAlmont. He used his Aunt's address to go to school in our district.

DeShon helped me through some tough times during my divorce. He's a good listener and always gives realistic advice, which is crazy because he has so much bad luck with women. In my opinion, he falls in love too fast, always rushing things. Relationships are like a good picture, they take time to develop.

He left the club last night with a girl, and by Sunday he'll think she's the one. After some good sex, and some decent pillow talk, his mind will be on a serious relationship with her.

Johnny Crew was a package car driver for UPS. He started there right after high school, and never looked back. UPS has been working that brother into the ground for almost ten years. "Ya'll candy asses can't work a real man's job," is what he told us all the time.

Of the four of us DeShon was the biggest. He was 6'6" and a rock solid 270lbs. He looks like a body builder. If you cross him, you better move your ass, because he is strong as an ox. In all reality, he's nothing but a big ole teddy bear eating porridge, looking for his momma bear. He loves the big sistas. He just can't find the right one. He says he wants a woman who's beautiful and comfortable with her weight. He says he's tired of seeing size 18 women wearing size 14 clothes. You can still look good in clothes that aren't too tight or too short. He makes good money and has some great benefits, so with some time and patience, he'll find someone.

Reggie Crew didn't go to college either. He owns a lawn care service and landscaping business. He was always the pretty boy of our little click. He used to tell us that he was proud of his Shemar Moore face and his LL Cool J body. So we never would have guessed he would make his living getting dirty using his hands. It was hard on him in the beginning but now he has a lot of regular clients and some big commercial contracts. It keeps him busy and keeps a very nice roof over his head. He and DeShon are the ones who have bought houses. Me and JC are still doing the apartment thing.

Reg wanted his own yard to play with. He had a bad break-up with his high school sweetheart, Michelle, several years ago. He has been bitter ever since. Reg is not looking for Mrs. Right, he's looking for Ms. Right Now. He plays a lot of games and breaks a lot of hearts.

The life he's living is gonna leave him old and lonely but you can't tell him nothing.

What goes around comes around.

DeShon

Sometimes, Some Things Just Feel Right

I got up this morning at about 8:30. Crystal was already gone. I don't know when she left. The liquor had caught up with me and had me in a coma. I said a Florida Evans triple damn when I realized she didn't leave her number. Before I took my shower, I could still smell her perfume on me and she was on my mind the rest of the day.

At practice one of my players told me that my mind seemed to be elsewhere. But they were happy because I let them go thirty minutes early. I was proud that a few of them stayed to work on their free throws.

Later that evening I was back at the house waiting to watch the finals of the preseason NIT. I made some cheese dip and bought some party wings from Chicken King on Pike Ave on the north side of town. Reggie and Johnny got there about seven thirty. Jason called and said he was running late. The game started at eight.

Reggie was headed straight for the food when he asked, "Where's Jason?"

"He called and said he'd be late. He was spending the day with Nyia. You know his schedule is about to get hectic, so he tries to spend as much time with her as he can."

"Yeah, between trying cases and running the streets, Monica don't spend any time with her."

"Man, JC, Jason told me the same thing. She needs to get her priorities in order. That little girl needs both her parents right now."

"Which one of those chickens did you leave with last night D?" That was Johnny.

"The one you gave all my info to nigga and she is not a chicken head."

"What did I tell her?" He said laughing.

"Man, you told her about Erica and everything."

"Damn Johnny, whenever you start drinking you run off at the mouth."

"I'm not trying to hear that Reg. He left with her didn't he? I must have said something right."

"So D, what happened last night? That girl was fine. Where did ya'll go?"

"We came back here."

"You hit it?" Reggie and Johnny asked in unison.

I smiled and said, "You guys know I don't kiss and tell."

"Bullshit nigga, you always bragging about the notches on your bed post."

"Naw, he don't kiss and tell when he really likes the chick. Ain't that right Reggie?"

"He's right D, she must have really put it on you."

"Let's put it like this, I haven't thought about Erica all day."

"Daamn!" That was both of them.

"She must have been off the chain, cuz Erica had you sprung."

"Reggie got you D, she did have your nose open pretty wide. She was there last night too."

"Who Erica? I didn't see her."

"She came in after you and ole' girl left. She was with Mike Stanley."

"Mike Stanley! She left *me* for *that* thugged out nigga?"

"Ya'll shut up about that tramp, the game is on."

Johnny agreed with him. I gave them both the finger. The game was the last thing on my mind at that point. Erica and Mike Stanley, now that's some bullshit. I treated her like the queen I thought she was and she fired me for a nigga who ain't about nothing. We grew up with Mike. We all knew he wasn't going to be about shit. He was a low class stick up kid who was in and out of jail. Why women like thugs I will never know.

"D, telephone." That was Reggie snapping me out of my trance. I didn't even hear it ring.

"Who is it?"

"It's some chick, the number came up private."

"Hello."

"Hey Sexy."

It was Crystal. "Hey Sexy? You must be looking in a mirror, talking to yourself."

"That line was pretty cute. I'll have to use that. How are you today?"

"I'm fine now. I was beginning to think I wouldn't hear from you again. How did you get my phone number?"

"Your friend Johnny, remember?"

"Figures."

I felt her smile. "Don't hit him, I'm just playing. Before I left, I dialed my cell from your phone so it would be on my caller ID."

"I see."

"Sorry I left like that, but I was feeling a lot of different emotions and I didn't want you to see me cry again."

"It was cool. I enjoyed having someone special in my arms. I'm here for you if you need me."

"Well I wish I could see you right now."

"What's stopping you?"

"You have company don't you?"

"Girl, just say the word and they outta here. We're just watching a basketball game."

"So you don't mind if I come over?"

"My door is always open for you."

"Okay, I will be there shortly."

I hung up the phone with a smile on my face. That thing about Erica and Mike was a distant memory. Crystal was all over my mind now.

"Okay boys, pack it up, time to go."

"It's not even halftime." That was Reggie with a mouth full of chips.

"What was that, a booty call? Can you believe this Reg? He's kicking out his boys on game night for some chick."

"Come on JC, you got to know by now I will kick ya'll to the curb for a female any day of the week. I would give up Super Bowl tickets to kick it with a female.

"I feel you D, but damn, Super Bowl tickets?"

"Well maybe not the Super Bowl, but you know what I mean."

"Well can we take the food?"

"Reggie, you can take it all as long as ya'll gone before Crystal gets here."

Just as they were walking out, Jason pulled up in his new ride. He told me about it on the phone but it looked better in person.

"The game over already?"

"Naw J, ya boy told us to kick rocks cuz that chick he left with last night is coming over. Unlock the door so I can check you out." Johnny said that and climbed in the passenger side. Reg got in the back seat.

"D, what you got going man? I just pulled up, it's probably not even half time yet."

"Sorry J-Rock, you know how it is when it comes to hot chicks, tell your boys to kick bricks."

Reg laughed. "It's kick rocks, dummy."

"I know that fool, I was trying to rhyme. J, man this truck goes hard man, I'm almost jealous."

"Yeah, this is phat, J. When you gonna let me borrow the keys?" That was Reggie.

"When you let me borrow some car notes."

I said, "J tell them what Nyia said about your new wheels."

He smiled and said, "Yea man she said my daddy driving a new red fire truck."

We all had a good laugh off that one. I said, "I guess she wasn't impressed by the Cadillac symbol."

"Alright man we'll go across town and watch the game at Hawgz Blues Café. I'm craving some of those award-winning smoked wings."

They all left and I started cleaning up the kitchen. When I finished, I lit a few candles and put Maxwell's "Urban Hang Suite" in the CD player. I turned the volume down to a whisper and sat down in front of the game. There were about two minutes left in the game when she knocked on the door. North Carolina was putting the smack down on Stanford.

I opened the door and she walked past me. Her sweet-smelling perfume was intoxicating. She was wearing a long sexy black dress and a nice leather jacket. I took her coat and hung it in the hall closet. When I turned around the long black dress was down around her ankles. No panties. No bra. The whole scene looked as if it was straight from one of those romance novels.

"If the look on your face is an indication of how bad you want me, come over here and show me."

I went over and kissed her. After another long kiss she said, "You trying to make me fall in love with you, aren't you DeShon?"

"I can tell by that look in your eye that you already love me," I said with a smile.

She chuckled a little and said, "You are so full of yourself."

"Well come a little closer so you can be full of me too."

My tongue eased back into her mouth and the sweet taste from last night was still there. I squatted a little and took one of her breasts in my mouth. I kissed and suckled her nipple as if I were a baby feeding for the first time. Then I switched to the other one so there would be no jealousy. I stood back up and gently pushed her up against the wall beside the couch. I grabbed one of the throw pillows off of the couch and kneeled down on it.

With her back firmly against the wall, I put her right leg on my shoulder. Her dugout wasn't nappy at all, she was cleanly shaven. I dove in, tongue first. I thought she was going to rip my ears off. As my tongue slid deeper inside her, she rose up a little and put her other leg on my shoulder. She was in midair with her weight on my shoulders as I licked her inside and out. I was trying to hit her G-spot with my tongue. Her juices were running down her thighs and I was right behind them making sure I tasted it all. I stood up and kissed her some more and she started undressing me. I felt comfort in her arms. Her kisses sent shock waves through my body.

There was a certain art to kissing and I guess you could call her Picasso. Our lips hugged and our tongues slow danced. When all my clothes were in a pile in the middle of the living room floor, I led her to the counter next to the kitchen table. She smiled and took the condom out of my hand. She called me the last Boy Scout as she bent down to put it on.

She stood back up and started to climb up on the counter. I stopped her and turned her around. She read my mind and bent over a little bit. I slid my key into her lock. I loved her from behind. She moaned and asked why I was doing her this way. She begged for me not to stop. There were no red lights or stop signs in my path. My green light turned yellow as I slowed down to sit her on the counter. The height of the counter was perfect as she spread her legs to welcome me back inside her. As I fell deep into her black hole, her nails pierced deeper into my back. We reached our intended destinations at the same time. I took her down off the counter and carried her into the bedroom. We got under the covers and kissed each other like it was our honeymoon.

"Why do I feel so safe with you DeShon?"

"Because I try to make you feel that way."

"But you really don't even know me.

"Sometimes some things just feel right."

I was lying on my back and she was beside me with her head resting on my chest. She was right, we didn't know anything about each other but I knew what made her special. It was the way she looked at me like she wanted me, like she really wanted to be with me. She was one of the sexiest women I have ever known. We all know sexy is not just a look. It's a look with a certain attitude, an attitude that she certainly had. I looked down at her face and she seemed deep in thought.

"What's on your mind?" I asked her.

"I was thinking that I wished we would have met a few years and a few relationships ago."

"You say that like there's a problem with us trying to get together now."

"No, it's not like that. What do you do for a living?"

"I'm the head basketball coach at Southwest Jr. High. What about you?"

"You're a coach at Southwest? How long have you been coaching there?"

"This is my third year. Why?"

"I'm just being nosy. We don't know each other right, so I'm just trying to get to know you."

"Well my life is a library book ready for you to check out and read."

After that, she started firing questions at me as if she were a prosecuting attorney. She asked me things about my parents, where I grew up and things like that. Then we talked about movies and music. That's all I remember before I fell asleep. When I woke up she was gone.

Damn, I sleep too heavy. I'm glad she's not a thief.

DeShon

Games People Play

I haven't heard from Crystal all day. I looked at my Caller ID for her number but I remembered she had hit *67 before she called. I still didn't know much about her, but she knew a lot about me. When I thought about it, she avoided most of the questions I asked her.

My dogs were going to poetry night at this new club called The Den over in the river market downtown. Little Rock needed a club like that. The club scene here is bad but it's getting better. I was going to ask Crystal did she want to go. It's almost seven now and the show down there starts at eight.

I went ahead and hit Johnny on his cell and told him I would meet them down there. After jumping in the shower, I scrubbed down with my Armani shower gel. The ladies love this Gio cologne and shower gel. I put on a navy-blue Sean John button down, a pair of jeans and some Tims. I looked in the mirror before I left and thought about that Outkast song and smiled - so fresh, so clean. I drove to the river market district with Crystal on my mind. I got there about fifteen till 9. I looked for a parking space and for Johnny's car on the club's lot. I found neither and had to park a little bit down the street. I was about to call Johnny when they pulled up behind me. I got out and sat in the backseat with Reg.

I needed to get a hit of whatever he was drinking. He was sipping on Crown and Coke. I really don't drink brown liquor but it was better than nothing. We all got out and headed for the club. They were clowning me about Crystal all the way to the door. I was everything from a pussy whipped schoolboy to a sprung sugar daddy. We each paid the ten-dollar cover and found a table. Johnny ordered some wings. This was a new spot so I would have to taste his before I spent my money. I looked up and seen this guy walking toward our table. He looked familiar.

"What's up Coach Bryson?"

"Hey what's going on?" I didn't know where I knew him from.

"I'm Myron Nelson's uncle. Remember, I used to pick him up from practice."

"Yeah, yeah, okay. Myron's doing good over at McClellan I hear."

"He is, but he said he wishes you were still his coach. My sister and I do too. You taught those kids a lot."

"Thanks man. I appreciate that. What was your name again?"

"Lorenzo, Lorenzo Thomas."

"So you came down to check out some poetry huh?"

"Yeah, the wife dragged me down here. We kinda been going through some things so we need this time together you know."

"I feel you. I hope ya'll enjoy the show."

"Well there she is coming out of the ladies' room. Let me get back to the table. It was good seeing you coach, stay up fellas."

We watched him head to his table to catch a glimpse at his wife. It's a guy thing. Our level of respect rises for you if you have a good-looking wife. His wife was fine. His wife was Crystal.

"Damn D, ain't that your girl?"

"Shut up Reggie, you talking too loud."

Johnny was right, he was talking loud. This was a fucked-up situation but some things were starting to make sense. She never gave me her number, she avoided my personal questions and she wanted to know how long I coached at Southwest. She had to be thinking that I probably knew her husband and his nephew. I must look like a Playstation because everybody was trying to play me.

My first thought was to get up and cause a scene but I know I'm bigger than that. I stood up and walked toward their table. I heard Reg laugh and say, "It's on now."

When Crystal finally saw me coming her way, she looked surprised. She shifted in her seat and I could tell she was uneasy. That was my intent. She looked at me like I was Tupac coming out of hiding. I walked up and started talking to Lorenzo.

"Hey man, before the show started I wanted you to tell Myron to give me a holla so I can know when they play next. My friend Jason is a scout for UALR. He's always looking for good local talent."

"Okay, I'll tell him to get you a schedule."

"Thanks, I try to take care of my boys when I can."

"Excuse my manners Coach, this is my wife, Crystal. Crystal, this is Myron's old coach, DeShon Bryson."

She looked up, tried to smile and said, "Nice to meet you."

I told her the same thing and went back to the table.

But I walked right past it and toward the front door. Again I heard Reggie's mouth. This time he said, "Don't let that bitch run you off."

I just kept walking. When I got outside and headed for the truck, I heard Crystal call my name. I stopped so she could catch up. She was wearing a brown leather skirt with matching boots and a cream-colored turtleneck sweater. Damn she looked good. Why do I always meet these fine ass triflin' women?

"DeShon, I am so sorry about all of this."

"Sorry about all of what? What is *this*?"

"Don't make this harder than it already is."

"Crystal, you can save this shit for Oprah cuz I ain't tryin to hear it."

"Just listen to me for a second."

"Listen to what? How he doesn't pay enough attention to you or how he cheated on you so you returned the favor? Oh I know, he ain't hittin' it right."

"I never meant to hurt you DeShon."

"You know, I'm sick of hearing people say that dumb shit to me. You never meant for me to find out. After what we shared you knew I would be hurt if I found out you were married."

"Look DeShon, what you and I shared was special to me and it seems to have been special to you. We shouldn't walk away from this angry."

This chick is crazy.

"You keep saying *this*, what the hell is *this* between us? It's nothing. You're married sweetheart. You said it right. What we did was special to me, past tense. I said emotions can't be turned on and off like a light but you hit the switch and blew out the bulb."

She looked me in my eyes and I guess they told her my words were real. She looked as if she had a lot more to say but all she could say was I'm sorry. She walked back to the club with tears in her eyes. I leaned back against somebody's car massaging my temples. I needed a cigarette and I don't even smoke.

Feeling dusted and disgusted, I went back to the club to get my drink on. When I walked in, I gave a head nod to my dogs to let them know that I was okay and went straight to the bar. I ordered me an Absolut and cranberry and a Bombay and tonic. I hit the gin fast and turned around when I heard a sweet-sounding voice call my name.

"Hey DeShon, remember me?"

I couldn't place her right off but then it hit me. "Keisha, right?"

"Right, we met at the Matrix the other night. You must have left right after we danced because I was looking for you."

"Yeah I did, something came up and I had to leave."

"Everything's cool I hope."

"Yeah, it turned out to be nothing. So, Ms. Keisha, who are you here with?"

"I'm with my sister, Trina. This poetry night is more my speed. The Matrix was cool but I'm really not a club person. My girls dragged me out that night."

"You sound like me. My homeboys done me the same way that night but the way you were moving on the dance floor, you seemed to be right at home." I said with a grin.

"I see you got jokes. Well if I was right at home, you was all up in my living room. Why don't you come sit with me so we can talk some more?"

"Sure, the show is on C.P. time so we have a little time to chit chat."

I paid for my drinks and followed her to her table. I stopped by my table and gave Reggie the Absolut. I wanted to keep my head clear. Keisha seems cool but this time I need to slow my ass down.

My heart can't take all the games people playing with my emotions.

Nicole

Won the Battle, Begin the War

It had been almost a month since Brandon and I had our lil episode in the car. He is too big for my belt. But our long talk, no DVD player or Xbox for 3 weeks got his attention. What really hurt his feelings was the fact he couldn't go to the basketball court down the street after he got in from school. I didn't even let him go on the weekend. That punishment hurt his behind more than any belt could have. He had to learn that he can't talk to me like I'm somebody off the street.

I learned a lot about his feelings toward John. He thinks he has done ok without him but wishes he had a male influence around. So for now he looked to his coaches for guidance. I pretty much had a grown-up conversation with my 12-year-old son. Our relationship got stronger after that night.

I enjoyed our ride home from the games because we talked all the way there. We would talk about his day and he would actually ask me about mine, I thought that was so sweet.

Brandon's team was undefeated after 8 games. He was simply amazing on that court. My son was clearly the best player on the team but this other boy Dion Camp was scoring almost 20 points per game. Brandon was filling up the stat sheet averaging 11 points, 8 assists, 5 rebounds and about 2 steals.

That big head boy Dion led the team in points and turnovers, he really got on my nerves. He plays no defense at all but Coach Anderson never says anything to him. Dion never gets yelled at when he makes mistakes like the other players. One night while Brandon was watching his game tapes and I was washing dishes, I asked him about Dion and the coach. Then I thought, he needed to be washing dishes while I watch TV.

"Brandon, the coach never yells at Dion, why is that?" He was on the ottoman eating my croutons like a bag of chips. He hates when I make salads for dinner but he loves my croutons.

"Well Dion's daddy and coach are good friends, that's why he never says nothing to him."

"Coach Anderson is going to ruin that boy."

"Too late Ma, that boy already gone. Everybody telling him how good he is and he believes all the hype."

"You're better than him."

"I know that. Coach and the rest of the team know it too."

"Well they don't act like they know."

"When we first started practicing and scrimmaging, Coach would put me and Dion on different teams. I was busting his ass every day, he couldn't guard me."

I frowned, "What makes you think you can curse in front of me?" He looked nervous.

"Sorry Ma, it just kinda slipped out."

I smiled and threw my dish rag at him, "It's cool this time but watch your mouth, or I'll wash that potty mouth out with this dish washing liquid."

"But seriously Ma, Coach knows he can't win without me or Dion."

Now I knew that this Coach Anderson had some issues. He showed me his true colors about a week later. I was in McCain Mall one Saturday afternoon, he approached me right after I got my order at the Pretzel Maker.

"How you doing Ms. Dade?"

"Oh hi Coach Anderson, just out getting my shop on." I said that as I held up my bags.

"I see that you have a Dillard's bag and shoes from Warren's. Where's the Victoria Secret bag at? I hear they having one helluva sale."

I didn't like where this conversation was headed. So I nodded toward his wedding ring and said, "I'm sure your wife would love something out of there."

"She has enough of that stuff already. I'm trying to buy you something. Of course, if I buy it I gotta see you in it"

I know I was looking cute in my burnt orange wool sweater, denim skirt, and a pair of Boss boots I got from Belk, but I wasn't looking for attention from this tacky bastard. Why would any woman in her right mind holla at a grown ass man still wearing a fanny pack? On top of all that he's got a wife at home. Looking like Uncle Junior from the Jamie Fox show ... trying to run his weak game on me.

"You know what coach I'm about to walk away and pretend this didn't happen."

When I turned around he grabbed my arm and pulled me back. When I snatched my arm away, he got too close up on me and said, "This *did* happen baby girl and you will regret it if you walk away."

Those high heel boots prevented me from flat out running from this pervert. I want to punch him in his face but I just need to get away. When I got to my car I was so angry I was shaking. This fool actually put his hands on me.

He let me know what he meant by regret at Brandon's next game.

We were playing at Dunbar Middle School. Brandon always gets a rest with about 2 minutes left in the 1st quarter. But after that the coach never put Brandon back in the game. Coach kept looking up at me with an ugly smirk on his face. Brandon sat at the end of the bench looking frustrated. I felt so bad for Brandon. We won the game because Dunbar's team wasn't any good. We had beat them pretty bad the 1st time we played them. Coach knew what he was doing, he knew he could win this game without my son. The man didn't have to do my baby like this. This fool wasn't gonna get away with this shit. After the game Brandon eased into the car, he was usually upbeat and hyper after his games.

"Ma, wassup with you and Coach?"

"Why you ask?"

"When I asked why he didn't play me for 3 whole quarters, he told me to ask you."

I told Brandon what happened in the mall. My Dodge Charger was our couch where we talked about our troubles of the day. I don't know why but I thought my 12-year-old son would understand what I had just told him.

"You telling me he put his hands on you."

"We'll just go to the principal or maybe even the school board. He's not going to do this to you."

"Ma, his brother is the principal and his wife is on the school board. They not gon' do nothing to that man. I got something for this nigga."

"*Jason* you know I don't like you using that word. We'll take our chances with the school board."

"Naw Ma, just let me handle it. I'm a good kid, right?"

"What?"

"Haven't I been a good kid?"

"Yeah, but..."

"Just trust me and let me handle it. We play the Bobcats Thursday. We will see if he does this to me again because they have a good team."

I didn't say anything. My baby was trying to be a man. I was proud and worried at the same time.

"You still love him don't you Ma?"

"What did you say? Love who?"

"Jason."

"Jason Hart? What has he got to do with any of this?"

"You called me Jason just now. You must still miss him. At times like this we need someone like him around."

I can't believe I called him Jason. But I have to admit Jason had been heavily on my mind since I found out Brandon was watching his game tapes. Brandon was trying to protect me just like Jason did all those years ago. I do miss him. And at times like this, I did wish I had him around.

Thursday night our team was playing the Horace Mann Bobcats. Mann was 1 game behind us in the conference standings. Brandon told me practice had been back to normal, but right before tip-off, the coach looked up at me and smiled. He grabbed Brandon and whispered something in his ear. Brandon just kinda smirked, shook his head, and walked to the end of the bench.

Then Coach went to Brandon backup, Freddie Walker, after Coach whispered in Freddie's ear, he jumped up off the bench with a smile on his face. When the announcer called out the line-ups Freddie was starting in place of Brandon. The fans sitting around me in the stands were asking me was Brandon hurt. But I was busy trying to get his attention. He finally looked up, he told me he was ok.

Steven "Chris" Ware

When the buzzer for the 1st period sounded, we were losing 26-11. Both Freddie and Dion were having terrible games. All the fans around me were in an uproar because Brandon wasn't playing.

Right before the start of the 2nd period Coach Anderson yelled for Brandon to check into the game. The crowd cheered when they saw my son stand and pull the shooting shirt over his head. When he walked toward the coach, he pulled his jersey off.

"Don't ever disrespect my mamma again, I quit."

Then Brandon headed up the bleachers toward me but not before throwing his jersey in Coach Anderson's face. I sat there in shock like the rest of the crowd. When Brandon sat down I said, "Let's go."

"Naw Ma let's stay till the end."

"Well step in the hallway and talk to me for a second."

As we walked out all eyes were on us.

"Brandon, why did you do that?"

"Ma, I'm not gonna play games with this dude. If we were winning he would have never put me in that game."

"This decision could hurt your future. I wish none of this mess ever happened."

"I'm ready to face the consequences of my actions. Now he has to explain when people start asking questions about what went down."

Actually my baby was right. I just grabbed him and hugged him real tight. He let go and said he was going to the locker room to change. By the time he came back out it was almost halftime and the score was 52-21.

A few parents came to us to ask what was going on. I just said it was a long story and we would fill them in another time. When the horn sounded for the intermission, Coach looked over his shoulder at us.

The look on his face let me know we had won the battle but I knew that this was the beginning of a war.

Jason

Master of Your Domain

With all that had been going down we needed a road trip. So I talked Johnny and DeShon into rolling down to Dallas this weekend. We would touchdown in Texas at least 4 times a year. Little Rock can get boring at times so we try to take as many road trips as we can. We never stayed in a hotel, we always stayed with Reggie and Johnny's cousin Chris. Chris had a nice house in Arlington. If you know anything about Texas, you know that Dallas, Fort Worth, and Arlington are all about 10 miles apart. So we kick it in those three cities the whole weekend. We would kick it like Klan members at a white sale.

Friday night we were at a club called Jamie's. If a brotha' didn't have on Ralph Lauren and a fresh pair of Jordans, he didn't get any play in that ghetto club. I had on both but the play I was getting from those hoodrats wasn't worth my time. I was having a good time but one chick I was dancing with smudged my white polo shirt with her ugly lipstick. I'm not violent, but for a moment I thought about treating her like her name was Anna Mae and I was feeling like Ike.

Saturday night was a little different. That night we went to a club called Rockafella. This club had a dress code and an older age limit, so it was a little more classy.

DeShon was standing right beside me when this fine sista walked past us. DeShon usually has the same taste in women as I do. So we have bumped heads in the past, it was friendly competition. He saw her first but I beat him to the punch because when he saw her he was just standing in awe. Her skin was a pretty brown, almost the color of a used penny. The hairstyle she was rocking made me think of Mary J. Blige in her "No More Drama" video. So I stepped around him and made my move. She was wearing some skin-tight leggings with a top that didn't go past her waist. Her body was looking so *bootylicious* in those pants it made that dumb ass song start playing in my head. Those leggings women wear make the smallest girl look like she has a plump ass. But this chick already was phat in the back, and she had me thinking thoughts that would probably get me slapped if I said them out loud.

"Hey sexy, are you feeling this song?" It was "Up Down" by T-Pain.

"What?"

"I asked are you feeling this song?"

"Why?"

"Because if you are let's dance. I only want to dance with you if you like the song, that way you will dance with some passion."

She smiled, "Why are you looking at me like that, are you nervous or something?"

"To be honest I'm a little nervous. Beautiful woman can be intimidating sometimes. I just want to dance to a song you enjoy listening to."

"First I was sexy. Now I'm beautiful. Which is it?"

"Both, you have a sexy body, and a beautiful face."

The next song that came through the speakers was "Pussycat" by Missy Elliot. She gave me a sneaky smile, grabbed my hand and escorted me to the dance floor. I'm not shy, but I think I kinda blushed. If I were a white boy my face probably would have been red. If you know the words to the song you will understand why.

When we got to the floor, she turned to face me. I pulled her sexy body real close and she put her arms around my neck. That made me feel good because if she were just being nice she would have kept her back to me the whole time. I was wearing a denim Sean John outfit. She pulled her arms from around my neck and put them inside my jacket around my waist. The soldier in my pants had been standing at full attention since she grabbed my hand. She felt it and looked down.

"I hope that's a flashlight in your pocket."

"Actually it is. I forgot to mention that I was a top-flight security guard. You look suspect. That's why I approached you."

"Well you were so busy looking at my sexy body and my beautiful face, that you forgot to ask me my name. You should be fired, toy cop."

"Ok pretty lady, what is your name?"

"My name is Porsha, and yours would be?

"The name is Jason. Porsha that's a nice name. I've always wanted to take one of those for a test drive."

"Well Porsha has a lot of horsepower. You think you can handle it all?"

As soon as she asked me that question the DJ played "Ignition" by R. Kelly. She was already laughing out loud when I said, "Well I am an experienced driver and the words of this song will tell you how I feel about everything else you were about to ask me."

We both laughed out loud as we walked off the dance floor. I went to the bar and ordered a Bombay and tonic. Porsha was right behind me like she was my girl. It made me feel good that she was so close to me.

"You want something?"

"Are you hoping that if you buy me a couple of drinks you'll get me to go home with you?"

"Damn Ms. Cleo, I thought you were for entertainment purposes only."

"Well if that's the case, I want a Leg Spreader."

"Leg Spreader? Is that really a drink?"

She stepped in front of me and told the bartender what she wanted. The bartender looked at both of us, smiled and started mixing her drink. Porsha was standing right in front of me. Then she turned and put her arms around me.

"So where do you stay?"

"Little Rock, Arkansas."

"That's a long drive. Can you bring me back in the morning?"

I smiled, "You would go all the way back to Little Rock with me?"

She looked down and said, "Yes, I'm dying to see the big black flashlight you keep poking me with."

"I don't have to take you across state lines. I'm staying with my homeboy in Arlington, unless you want to kick it at your place."

"No, sweetheart I live in the hood. I don't want you to get shot at."

"I'm from the hood myself, I'll shoot back. Where you from, Oak cliff?"

"You know it. What you know about Oak cliff?"

"My friends and I come this way all the time. My man Reggie met a girl from Oak cliff last summer."

"What's her name?"

"Carla"

"Carla Hansberry?"

"Hell I don't know her last name. She wasn't my girl."

"Does she play basketball?"

"Yeah, She's kinda tall."

"I know her. We went to high school together. We were on the track team together."

"Cool, so who are you here with tonight?"

"Just a few girls I go to school with."

"Why don't we all go back to my friend's house and hang out?"

"That's cool with me, but I'm gonna let you know this up front. I'm here to kick it with you. I just met these girls this semester, so I really don't know a whole lot about them. Your boys are on their own."

"Boo I don't care if they make a love connection or not. You're the only one I care about right now."

She gave me a kiss on the cheek as we grabbed our drinks and headed to the table where her girls were sitting. To my surprise all of them looked pretty good. When you are dealing with a group of girls, one of them usually looks like Aunt Esther.

My dogs were still on the dance floor. After sitting there a few minutes, looking at faces and listening to these girls talk, I knew who would hook up with whom. I knew DeShon would talk to this girl Ashley because she was the prettiest. He would be sitting right next to her when the introductions were made. Porsha's friend Tonya was very talkative and damn near ghetto. Her conversation made me think she had some hoodrat tendencies and she was pleasantly plump. So I knew her and Johnny would hook up, because the other girl wasn't saying much. Her name was Chanel. Chris, who is rather shy himself, would have to chop it up with her.

Porsha was telling them about going to Chris's house when my boys walked up to the table. Introductions were made, and everything popped off like I thought it would. We all laughed and talked for a hot second then called it a night. When we got outside Tonya leaned over to try to whisper something to Porsha. She had been drinking and we all know drunk folks can't whisper.

"Girl, I hate it that I couldn't find the nigga who is pushing that red Escalade we saw coming in."

"Please, that dude probably sell more dope than the Mexican cartel."

I asked, "So every nigga with a tight ride is a hustla?"

Porsha said, "Most of the time."

I got close to my truck, pulled out the keys and hit the alarm. All four of them stopped.

DeShon said to Tonya, "Sorry sweetheart, you didn't meet the nigga pushing the Cadillac truck, she did." He pointed at Porsha as the four of us busted a gut laughing.

"This is *your* truck?" That was Ashley.

"Si, senorita. The cartel sent me down here to check on our business here in Dallas."

Everyone laughed except Porsha, who was standing there with a disapproving look on her face.

"I'm just bullshitting. This is my trunk but I don't sell dope. I can't say I haven't thought about it because the notes on this thing are a muthafucka."

I was talking to everyone but I was looking into Porsha's eyes. She walked closer to the truck and gave me a little smile. I pulled her close and gave her a big hug.

I gave Chris the keys and headed to the other side of the truck. I had been drinking, and Chris is always the designated driver. The girls piled into Tonya's Honda

Civic, which was parked about two rows over from us. The guys were talking about how fine the girls were when I fell asleep. The liquor had got the best of me. I slept all the way to the house.

"Jason, wake yo' ass up dude, we almost at the house." That was Johnny.

DeShon said, "Yeah, man you over there snoring and everything. You better hope Patrice don't try to kiss you when you get out of the truck, cuz I know your breath is hot and tart right now."

"Her name is Porsha dude, you always forgetting these girl's names. Do you remember your girl's name?"

"It's Allyson, right?"

"Hell naw, its Ashley. You gonna get all these ladies riled up if you call her the wrong name."

Johnny pushed Chris in the back of the head. "Dude you better not fall asleep."

"Hey, keep yo hands off me, before I flip the bitch over and kill us all."

"Wreck your own ride, I pay ..."

DeShon said, "We know, we know. You pay too much money to them folks for this thing every month. Yada, yada, yada we have heard it all before."

We all laughed as we pulled into the driveway.

The ride back to Dallas gave me a chance to sober up a little bit. It was about a 25-minute ride to Arlington. When I got inside I went straight to the bathroom to brush my teeth. I didn't want Porsha to think I had a problem with halitosis. I came out and saw that Chris, Johnny and their dates were at the kitchen table getting ready to play a game of spades. Porsha was on the couch watching music videos on T.V. She had to be watching Uncut on BET, because all I saw were big asses in thongs gyrating on the screen. I sat down beside her and kissed her on the cheek.

"Where did Ashley and DeShon run off to?"

"They walked down to the park at the end of the street."

"I see, do you want to play the winners next game?"

She smiled, "I didn't come here to play cards."

I stood up and extended my hand to raise her up off the couch. I led her by the hand to the back bedroom and closed the door. Before I could say anything, she clicked off the light and pushed me against the door. She got up real close and pressed her lips up against mine. Her tongue eased in my month. I could taste the fruity lip-gloss she was wearing. She reached for my shirt and pulled it over my head. I did the same thing to her, and undid her bra. Her cup size was about a C, she had the prettiest brown breasts I had ever seen. We fell back on the bed, and I was kissing her all over. I took each breast in my mouth and was turned on by her wiggling and moaning. Slowly her body stopped moving, and the moaning died out. I stopped to look up at her. Soft tears were rolling down her face.

"What's wrong baby?"

"I'm sorry Boo, I'll be o.k." She grabbed my hand. "Let's finish what we started."

She was trying to keep a smile on her face, and wipe away the tears, but she was fighting a war that had already been lost. The tears continued to fall.

"You are not ok. I'm a good listener, tell me what's on your mind." There was a moment of silence, and then she poured her heart out to me.

"I'm not really a club person. I go once a month, sometimes once every two months. But it seems like every time I go I end up going home with some guy. Does that make me a hoe? Cuz I feel like one right know."

I pulled her close so she could rest her head on my chest. "Some people may look at you that way but I wouldn't."

"Please, you're just saying that because I'm lying here with you half naked. If we had finished what we started, you would have rode back to Arkansas talking about the hoe you met at the club. And how you fucked her the same night."

"That's not true at all, honestly I kinda like you. I was hoping after tonight we could keep in touch. I come to Texas a lot, so I thought you and I can kick it when I come in town."

She sat up in the bed. "That exactly the kinda shit I'm talking about. You want me to be the piece of ass you get to see when you go on vacation or something. You probably got a girl back home wondering if you are staying true to her. You ain't shit."

That hurt my pride a little bit, actually it pissed me off. She was up looking for her shirt and bra. "Look Porsha, don't you sit here and judge me. You don't even know me. Think about it, if all I wanted from you was some ass I wouldn't be sitting here listening to you. I would be trying to convince you that everything is all right and that we could still do it. That's not what I am about. So how about we put our clothes back on and talk. We can talk like adults, cuz I'm not gonna stand here and let you call me a triflin' nigga trying to get you out of that thong."

She finished hooking her bra, and sat back on the bed. She leaned over and wrapped her arms around my neck. I felt her warm tears rolling down my shoulder. I sat there with mixed emotions. There was no doubt that I wanted to have sex with her. But I sure didn't want her feeling like she was less than a woman if we slept together. So I told her my thoughts. She gave me half a smile and said, "Thanks for being honest with me. If you were not a gentleman, this would have been my third one-night stand in the past six months."

"But it wasn't planned that way right, you went home with the guy thinking it would lead to something more right?"

"Right, we would have fun that night and then exchange numbers. When I called they were always busy and when they called me, it was always late, asking me to come over."

"Only booty calls, huh?"

"Yep, only booty calls."

"Well when I call it will be long distance, but I will hop on a redeye if you need me to come rub the booty." She looked up at me with a big smile on her face.

"There's that pretty smile I saw at the club. Well I guess you can say that I'm master of my domain. I got my hormones in check so let's put the rest of our clothes on and play some cards or something."

"Master of your domain. I see you watch Seinfeld."

"I watch the reruns every night at 6:30. I love that show."

"Me too, but it comes on at 5:30 here. I'm really not into cards, so let's go down to that park. It's four 0'clock in the morning, do you think you can protect me from the muggers and dope fiends?"

Steven "Chris" Ware
153

"This is a pretty decent neighborhood, so I hope we don't have to worry about none of that. But if push comes to shove, I promise I won't leave you behind if we have to run."

She laughed and said, "I run a 12 flat in the 100-meter dash, so I know you won't leave me behind."

When we were fully dressed I opened the bedroom door. I heard the headboard banging the wall in the next room. I got to the kitchen table and the same foursome was there. So that meant DeShon and Ashley were bumpin' and grindin' in the other bedroom. They will be in love in the morning.

Porsha and I headed out the front and walked to the park. I stood in between her legs as she sat at the edge of a picnic table. We were out there chatting and kissing. We talked about things we had in common. Like the fact we both grew up in the hood, and all the drama we both been having in our love lives.

We talked until the sun came up.

We walked back to the house holding hands like two high school kids. I hated having to come home to Little Rock, because I was already looking forward to coming back.

Nicole

Typical Questions

I was sitting at a booth at TGI Friday's waiting on my girls. It had been months since we had hung, the 1st time since I've been back in Little Rock. Tiffany was in town for the week from Dallas. LaSha was headed here from work.

The vodka was strong in the Appletini I was drinking.

Tiffany and LaSha were classmates. I had met Tiffany back in the day when she dated Jason's best friend DeShon. I can't wait to tell her DeShon is Brandon's coach. I know she still has strong feelings for him. She hadn't had a real relationship since he cheated on her before they left for college.

LaSha is a different story when it comes to men. In my opinion she opens her heart and legs way too early with these guys. She doesn't ask enough questions. They usually end up being married or have a girlfriend they forgot to mention. And she is always so devastated when she finds out the truth. Last night she was telling me about this new guy, but I see flaws already. He never answers his phone when she calls, he always calls her back. She doesn't even know where he stays or where he works.

Makes me think he's Tommy from Martin, "He ain't got no job man!"

I look toward the door and see the Divas ask the hostess about me. The strawberry blonde pointed them in my direction. I couldn't contain my smile as my girls headed my way. Jazzy as always, Tiffany was dressed to impress with a Gucci hobo bag on her arm. Gorgeous is one of many flattering words I would use to describe her. Caramel brown skin, shoulder length dreadlocks, she makes all the guys pause when she enters any room. But she was surprisingly very humble, females with her looks and style were usually conceited beyond control.

LaSha was very pretty also. She was dark brown and has worn a short hairdo for as long as I've known her.

"I was about to eat without ya'll. Somebody paying my bill for making me wait."

"Well that's gonna have to be Miss Gucci purse right here, she the one balling!"

"Don't hate cuz I got swag Boo-Boo. Nicole stand up and give me a hug girl. It seems like forever since I seen you."

"I know girl, you need to move back to Arkansas so I can see you all the time."

"Okay, me and Nicole need you here for girls night out. You know we need you to be the ref when me and her old ass get together."

"There you go with the old jokes, we only 5 years apart."

"Dog years baby, dog years!"

"You calling me a bitch?" I said with a smile.

"Boy, ya'll stay on one." That was Tiffany.

"We just be playing. Sha know I love her like an evil step-sister. She needs to finish telling me about this new prince charming."

"I gave him some last night, and it was good too."

Tiffany started shaking her head, "Already, Sha? You be taking yourself way too fast."

I said, "Not really this time. She has known him for a while but she doesn't know much about him. He got too many secrets for me."

"For you? He's my man, and it ain't no secret he knows how to take me there!"

Tiffany said, "How do you feel about this guy?"

"I like him a lot, I'm not in love yet but I'm close."

I asked, "How does he feel about you?"

"I think he feels the same way about me."

I went on. "Last night when ya'll did the nasty, were you naked?"

"Of Course."

"Was he?"

"Yes he was naked, besides his wife-beater."

"He kept his wife-beater on? That's a red flag right there. It's a subconscious thing. If he doesn't take off all his clothes, it means he's holding back."

"Wow, Nic I haven't heard that one. Is that true?"

"T you know she just be talking, Nic, you be trippin."

"It's not true in all cases, but it can be. Think about the men you've both been with and if they took off all their clothes the first time you gave up the goods. It's almost as if they took off all their clothes they're obligated to stay or something. They leave some clothes on so it's easier to get up and leave. I just said it was a red flag,

I'm not saying he's not going to be a good man. I'm just saying guard your heart."

"Nic, you know me and you have had our battles in the past, but I hear you this time. I'm sitting here thinking about men in my past and our sexual escapades. There could be some truth in what you're saying. And for the record I always guard my heart."

Tiffany asked, "How so?"

"Think about it. Although I do fall in love fast for most of these guys, I know when to let go and move on. I've never been engaged to nor had a baby by any of those sorry men I've been with. I just want a good man and to start a family. That's not too much to ask, so why is it taking so long?" Tears were rolling down her cheeks.

Tears are as contagious as any disease and LaSha had infected me and Tiffany. We huddled up and hugged. I never saw this emotional side of Sha. I was always hard on her about her choices in men, but she was right she never stayed too long, she always knew when to let go.

I had to respect my girl for that. Sha let go and started wiping mascara from her cheeks. The waitress came and took our order.

"Damn T, I said I want a good man, not a woman. You hugged up on me like you want me. Seems like you need a man more than me."

We all shared a laugh. "Girl please, don't flatter yourself. I don't need a man in my life right now. I got too much going on."

"Whatever, I bet you don't be saying that at night."

"You right about that Sha, we all get lonely some nights."

"Hell yeah Nic, so Tiffany you still think about DeShon taking care of you on those lonely nights?"

"Where did that come from?"

"I'm with Nic. Where did *that* come from? How you just gon bring him up outta the blue?"

"I saw him on the news the other night, he's coaching over at Southwest Middle School."

"I know Brandon goes to school there, he's on the team."

"So you've seen him Nic? Why didn't you say something to me about it?"

Me and Sha looked at each other shaking our heads. "Well, the last time we were together, Nic brought up DeShon's name to you, and I recall you biting her head off, telling her not to talk about him around you. That's when we knew you still were in love with him."

"I'm not still in love with him."

"So you don't care that he asked about you when I enrolled Brandon in school?" Tiffany sat back in her chair at full attention. She couldn't hide her excitement.

"What did he say?"

"He just asked had I heard from you, how were you doing, the typical questions."

"Is he seeing somebody?"

Sha laughed, "Why do you care? I thought you weren't still in love with him?"

"I'm just asking."

"He didn't say. And I definitely didn't ask. I just told him that you were cool, living in Texas. He told me to tell you that he asked about you."

Sha said, "So you didn't ask about DeShon's personal life but did you ask about Jason's?"

"Yeah Nic, while ya'll on my case about D, have you talked to Jason since you've been back in town?"

"No I haven't, and I don't need to, that man is married."

"No, he's not."

"Sha, Jason has been married for a few years now. You told me that yourself, remember?"

"And I also told you he was divorced."

"I know she called and told me when it was listed in the paper."

"Sha, you never told me he was divorced. I didn't know. When did that happen?"

Sha smiled, "T you hear that? Nicole pussy just got wet! It's been a few months, so you got another shot at him. Neither one of ya'll can deny that you're still in love with those men."

"Well I can only speak for myself. I'm not in love with DeShon. I admit I think of him from time to time but I'm not in love with that man."

DeShon

The Square Root of 99

The pay-per-view fight was over and most of my guests had left. Reggie, Jason, and Johnny were still lounging around. Less than an hour ago my living room was packed with other coaches and friends watching Floyd Mayweather Jr put a serious beat down on Andre Berto. My regular crew was still hanging out giving Reg details of our lil road trip to Texas. I really needed that trip. I met *Ms. Right Now* while we were there.

Thinking about Ashley and that freaky encounter we shared had a smile on my face as I cleaned up the apartment. Ashley was a quick fix to the problem that is my love life. She was sexy and smart but lived too many miles away. I was buzzed from the vodka and cranberry, so my mind was all over the place. Ashley wasn't the only female on my mind, thoughts of Tiffany Martin were swirling through my head also.

She had been on the brain a lot since Nicole enrolled Brandon at the school. Nicole and Tiffany were still close after all these years. She told me Tiffany had been living in the DFW area since grad school. If I had that info while we were in Texas maybe I would have tried to look her up.

But Tiffany hadn't said two words to me since high school. Nicole dumped Jason right before the prom, and a big misunderstanding caused Tiffany to walk away from me. And she never looked back, she didn't even speak to me at graduation. What could have been has always been in the rear of my mind when it comes to Tiffany. Maybe my relationship trouble goes all the way back to her because we never got closure and I've secretly regretted it ever since.

"D, what was that chick's name you left the club with?" Johnny's loud ass snapped me back to reality.

"I know you trying to crack a joke but I remember her name it was Tiffany."

Jason and Johnny laughed real hard. Jason stopped enough to say, "Her name was Ashley fool."

"That's right, Ashley. Ain't that what I said?"

"Na, you said Tiffany. What's on ya mind or should I say who's on ya mind?" Jason had read me, he knew my mind was elsewhere. I didn't wanna talk about Tiffany in front of these drunk clowns right now, so I got the conversation off me.

"We need to talk about that fine sista you jacked from me bruh."

"Jacked? Don't be mad at me cuz you move too slow. While you were standing there admiring, I was headed to talk to her."

"She needed a lil mo meat on her bones for me. But I must say she was hella sexy, she definitely stood out."

As Johnny finished his statement, Reggie made a face as to say he wasn't impressed. Then he looked over at

Jason and asked did he hit it. So Jason gave him the same explanation he gave us on the ride back home.

Reg just started laughing, "That figures."

Jason cut his eyes over at Reggie, "What's that supposed to mean?"

"Never mind." The tension between Reggie and Jason has been on the rise the past few months. So I tried to change the subject back to the fight we just watched, so I won't have one in my living room.

But Jason wasn't having it. "Dead that D, Reg act like he got something to say. If it's on ya mind gone and get it off ya chest."

"You really don't wanna hear what I got to say."

"Nigga I'm all ears."

Johnny looked at me and I know he was thinking the same thing, this was about to get ugly.

Reggie verbally lit into Jason. "First of all nigga, when it comes to women, you a joke. Yo lil soft ass neva get no pussy. A bitch screw you over and you be right fucked up for years at time. And you still being nice to these broads, you need to man up."

Jason just sat there and shook his head, "Soft? Reggie you ain't half the man I am. If I'm a joke, nigga you the punch line. Don't judge me, you ain't shit."

Reggie stood up.

Johnny jumped up in front of his cousin. "Yo chill cuz. Damn man we all boys. All this ain't even necessary."

"Na, fuck that. This nigga need to hear this. Half the man you are? Please, I'm all the man these hoes need. I'm just like the nigga who fucked yo wife. Giving 'em what they missing at home."

That was all the way to the left. Because if I was Jason, I would have hit Reg with a left hook to the jaw after that. But the scary thing was Jason was cool, he actually kinda smiled. His whole demeanor was disturbing with all that was going on.

Jason stood up and said, "Reggie you ain't no man. All you do is find weak minded, insecure women. You got your heart broke and been scared of commitment ever since. But yet you still bitching and crying like a lil kid cause you can't trust a female."

"I know this nigga didn't just call me a bitch."

"No dumb ass. I actually called you a lil kid. But it you feel like a bitch, you might just be one, *bitch.*"

Reggie lunged at Jason but Johnny and me grabbed him before he got to him. Reg was hysterical screaming he was gonna kick Jason's ass. Jason was still standing there cool as ice, too cool if you ask me. "Johnny, D, let him go. He say he wanna kick my ass let him go. Better yet, step outside. I wanna see you kick my ass."

Jason opened the back door to what led to my backyard. We were struggling to hold back the raging bull that was Reggie. I told him that we all been tight, too long for it to go down like this.

"D's right cuz, let it go man, ya'll boys."

"Fuck that, this nigga need some act right, and I'm gone give it to him."

Me and Johnny stepped outside before Reggie. Jason was standing at the far end of the patio with his shirt off. The look in his eye had me nervous. The man who I called my best friend since grade school had pure evil in his eyes. Reg stepped onto the patio and looked up at Jason. He must have saw the same thing in Jason's eye that I saw because he hesitated.

"All this shit I've been going through the past few months: I lost my wife, lost my daughter. My life is fucked up. Then someone who supposed to be my boy, have my back, says some off the wall shit to me. I'm bout to let out some frustration all up in yo ass right now."

"You know what Jason, fuck you." Reggie turned and went back inside.

A few seconds later we heard my front door slam. Jason grabbed his shirt as he headed toward the backdoor.

"Sorry if I disrespected your house D. Johnny be glad your cousin walked away. I got to get outta here."

I made an unanswered request for Jason to stay and calm down, but he strolled past us back into the house. He grabbed the half empty bottle of Bombay Sapphire gin and walked out the front door.

Me and Johnny just stood there confused like someone asked what was the square root of 99.

Jason

It's About to Go Down

I t was shortly after midnight when I floated into Club Discovery. I say floated cause the gin had me on an inebriated high. My eyes were red and tight because of that good buzz. My mind was all over the place after my confrontation with Reggie. All the drama I've been dealing with the past few months, I didn't need one of my good friends coming at me like that. I got a lil too personal with him also. My temper and emotions got the best of me because I was ready to hurt someone who been a good friend half my life. I gotta make that right but that drama is secondary to my mission at hand.

Club Discovery or The Disco as it was mostly called, was a night club where a lot of gay couples and swingers hang out. It was famous for entertaining drag queen shows and concerts, great party atmosphere, and lots of beautiful, uninhibited women. The latter was my reason for being here.

I was a virgin to the spot and I was by myself so I didn't know what to expect. After I paid the $10 cover, I looked to my right and saw a woman who had to be at least 6'5" wearing a silver sequenced dress. Not only was she tall, she was built like Jon Cena. As I moved closer I realized *she* was actually a *he* when I saw that Granny Smith poking out of his neck. That scene almost made me say to hell with this and run outta here, but I was on a mission.

The fire in my loins was driving me deeper into this dark cave of wonders. Linkin Park was blasting the speakers as I entered the double doors to my left. As I walked through the club I was checking out my surroundings. Straight ahead there was two sexy Latinas kissing the French way. On my right, two white guys were doing the same thing. I kept it moving to the next room where Ludacris was telling bitches to move out the way.

The bar was mad busy with 4 female bartenders serving up the liquid courage. I found an opening, stepped up and ordered a Corona with extra limes. A caramel skin sista in a tan halter top and designer jeans came in beside me and ordered two white wines. She glanced over her shoulder at me and smiled. I smiled back as I looked closer at her neck to make sure there wasn't any forbidden fruit. Head to toe this lady was as fine as the wine she just ordered. As she leaned over on the counter waiting for her drinks, her body gracefully moved to the hip-hop music.

"When you finish your wine would you like to dance?"

She turned to face the voice that was behind her requesting her presence on the dance floor. She checked me out head to toe just like I had done to her, then asked for my name. When I told her, she turned and backed her ample backside up to my growing manhood.

"Jason, you see that tall, sexy sista watching us over there by the double doors? I'm with her."

The lady in question was way across the room but I didn't have to see her neck to know she was all woman.

She was just as sexy as the goddess standing in front of me. She was playing it close and had my nature rising like Jack's beanstalk.

"Well I wanna dance with your friend too."

"Jason that was the perfect answer. Pay for these drinks and meet us over there." I did as I was told and headed toward the double doors.

"Jason this is Tracy, Tracy this is Jason."

Tracy reluctantly stuck her hand out to shake mine and gave me a dry hello.

"So Ms. Dereon, you know my name, I know her name, but I still don't know who you are."

"Sorry my name is Dawn. I see not knowing my name didn't stop you from reading the tag on my butt."

"Hey I like reading stuff like that especially before I go to bed."

Tracy rolled her eyes and said, "That was real corny Jason. And where is your wife?"

"I can admit that was a little corny but hey, I'm drunk! And I only got 1 baby mamma, no bitch, no wife."

"Lord, now he's quoting rap songs."

"Chill T, don't front. We were just listening to that Jeezy song on the way here a lil while ago."

The look on Tracy's face and her body language let me know she didn't care for me too much. But Dawn was feeling me.

"Yeah Tracy chill, maybe what he's talking about in the song is what you need."

"You wanna be the one to beat this pussy up, nigga please."

"Lighten up sweetie, it was just a joke. It's the alcohol, don't take me serious."

Dawn felt the tension between me and her friend so she took me by the hand and led me to the dance floor.

"You have to excuse her, she's extremely jealous."

"It's cool, I understand. I'm drunk and I came here tonight looking for two beautiful women to go home with me."

"Wow, Jason does alcohol make you this honest and direct? That was bold."

"I'm sorry. Let me leave, I'm being disrespectful."

When I turned to leave, she pulled me back and kissed me. Her tongue eased in my mouth and danced a slow groove. She took a step back, looked me in my eyes and told me that her and Tracy were looking for a sexy gentleman to go home with them. She put her arms around my neck and started slowly grinding on me. I looked up and saw Tracy watching us. With my head I motioned for her to come join us. When she took the first step toward us, I kissed Dawn again. Tracy walked up and got right behind Dawn. Dawn bent over and wiggled her ass up on Tracy's crotch. She held on to Dawn's hips just like I would have if I were in her position. Tracy seemed to be more relaxed now that Dawn was grinding on her. Booty like that can ease anyone's pain.

Dawn stood up straight and moved behind her friend. I reached out to Tracy's hips and pulled her closer to me. Her eyes were telling me she didn't want me touching her but her body was moving like there was no other place she wanted to be. I started kissing her neck, she moved closer than close as I tilted my head and kissed her lips. Our tongues touched, and I felt her body loosen up a little more. When we stopped kissing, we opened our eyes and she gave me an approving smile, the whole scene was sexy.

Tracy turned around and started kissing Dawn. She also had on a pair of expensive House of Dereon jeans. Her backside wasn't as thick as Dawn, but it was big enough for me to admire her roundness. Tracy grabbed her friend's hand and started toward the front door. I hesitated because I was too turned on to think straight.

Dawn looked over her shoulder at me, then nodded for me to follow. That nod was a Bill Gates gesture because it made me feel like a million bucks.

I followed them to the parking lot.

They were parked close to the front in a white Lexus. I told them to meet me downtown at the Marriott. We needed to go somewhere close because I was still buzzing from the liquor.

I was leaving with two beautiful women. It was about to go down.

Jason

Dreams

Naked and confused, I was staring out the window as two sexy women slept in my rented bed. I gazed at the stars, thinking about my personal life and how much it was in disarray. Alcohol really is a depressant because I was down off my high, and feeling miserable about my situation. My self-pity party was interrupted when I felt erect nipples on my back. I didn't have to turn around to know it was Dawn with her arm around my waist. Her cucumber melon scent was soothing. Tracy smelled like Ur, Usher's fragrance for women.

She asked, "What on your mind? I hope not regrets."

"No regrets, just a lot of drama in my life right now."

"Well there a big couch over there and I'm a good listener."

I nodded toward the bed, "You not worried about waking your friend?"

"Wine, weed and an Ecstasy pill has her out like a light. Plus, you put it on her pretty good, she's good for a while."

"She was really on one."

As I turned from the window and headed toward the couch, Dawn saw my soldier standing at full attention. She was looking down at my manhood smiling big, "Looks like you have more than drama on your mind."

"It's been that way ever since you put those C-cups on my back."

"So you think you know my bra size."

"Sweetheart, after the all things I did to you in that bed over there, you're surprised that I know something as simple as a bra size?"

"Point taken."

When I sat down on the couch, Dawn went to the closet and grabbed one of the extra blankets. Then she cuddled up with me with her back to my chest. As her body got settled in, she leaned back and kissed me. A slow, sexy kiss like she belonged to me.

"Now tell me what's troubling you."

So I did just that.

I opened up to a stranger that I only knew biblically. I told her about my marriage and divorce, and how those events had affected me. How the loneliness and the bitterness toward women led me to sleep with almost 50 women in the past 6 months.

"What, did you just say almost 50 women in 6 months?"

"Unfortunately, yes."

"Wow, I was feeling kinda special until now. But I guess a lot of other women have experienced the same pleasure."

"I had sex a lot but not like we just did, but I used a condom all the other times."

"We did just play a dangerous game to fulfill our sexual desires. May I ask where you are meeting all these free-spirited women?"

I told Dawn about my recruiting job. On my business trips I was in the local bars, leaving with a new lady each time. We would go back to my hotel, a secluded area or sometimes we wouldn't make it out of the parking lot. On the weekends I didn't have Niya, I was at the bars and clubs. They knew me as Derrick Dunlap and I barely remembered any of their names. It felt as if I was trying to fill a hole or void that my ex left me with.

"I really miss being married, but I don't miss my wife, if that makes any sense."

"It makes perfect sense to me. I have been exactly where you are, without all the sleeping around of course. I suppose I was trying to fill my void by sleeping with a woman."

Steven "Chris" Ware
189

My eyes wondered to the bed. "How long have ya'll been together?"

"We are not officially a couple." Dawn turned and stared at the sleeping beauty in the bed as well. "If she had her way, we would be a couple. But I'm just not ready to give her all of me, you know?"

"I understand, sex with her is cool but you still desire a man's touch."

"It's amazing how observant you are, that's a rare quality in a man. At least all the men I know."

"I just try to read people. Eyes and body language tell a lot about a situation. I could tell you were eager for me to join the party, but Tracy, not so much."

"She only agreed to do it because I've been begging her to. Before tonight only one man had penetrated her, and you were the only one she gave permission to. She sacrificed a lot for me tonight."

Dawn went on to tell me how when Tracy was 13, her father's childhood friend and drinking buddy raped her.

"He was at their house drunk, said he was going upstairs to the bathroom but instead crept into her bedroom. Her daddy didn't believe her but her mother did. It got ugly between her parents, so they eventually moved out. But her mother treated her bad because she resented her for the situation like it was Tracy's fault. She still loved her husband. Her father kept drinking and drank himself into an early grave when she was 15. Her mother's lonely heart gave out two years later. Tracy was placed in foster care after that. She has lived a hard life."

I asked, "Does she hate men?"

"I don't think so because if she did, what we all did tonight would not have happened. She's just not attracted to men like she is women from what I can tell. After she turned 18 she slept with her female DHS case worker. She's only had sex with women from then till now."

Dawn went on to tell me about her marriage and divorce to a verbally abusive man, a man who tried to kill her self-esteem whenever he had the chance. He was a successful businessman who only wanted her to be a successful businessman's wife. She was just to be seen and not be heard. When she met James Moore, he was a sweet, confident man. Her friends and family must have saw something she didn't because all of them disapproved of him. But she loved him and ignored their warnings. He changed almost immediately after they said 'I do.'

She graduated law school a few months after the wedding so then he began to tell her she was too dumb to ever be a good lawyer and she would never pass the bar exam. He wanted her to stop living in a fantasy world, quit her pursuit of being an attorney so she could have his baby. She wanted kids but had no intentions of becoming a stay at home mom. Even after Dawn passed the bar on the 1st try, he still wasn't supportive of her.

She said it was by the grace of God they didn't have kids because she found out he had a mistress. Then one morning after an argument over him staying out all night, he punched her in the face. He only hit her once but that was one time too many for Dawn. She packed what she could the next day and never looked back.

Tracy was her divorce lawyer.

Dawn wiped tears from her eyes, "I was broke, so I slept with Tracy because I couldn't afford the attorney fees."

"Sometimes you gotta do what you gotta do."

Dawn slapped my leg, "That was a joke homie, I was just trying to lighten the mood."

I laughed, "Hey you don't seem like the type, but you never know!"

"But she did help me through a really rough time. I loved him and our relationship was great at first. It just got to a point where I was very unhappy, and had to make a difficult decision. When he hit me, it just sealed the deal."

"I know all about making difficult decisions."

"Tracy never bashed my ex-husband, and she had every right to. But all she did was be there for me, financially, emotionally and then sexually. She could be a perfect mate but I'm not ready to fully commit to a woman. Especially with men out there who could put it down like you."

"Not men ... me. You won't find too many men who will do you like I just did."

"You're probably right. Me and James had a good sex life, at least I thought we did. In my mind everything was good in the bedroom, until I met his chick on the side. I saw her, she was cute but she had a couple of kids and lived in the projects. Why would a successful married man want to be with her?"

"Well you have to look at it like this, you are an extremely beautiful, intelligent woman. It would be hard to find a woman like that to cheat with a married man."

"I see where you're coming from to a certain extent. But the girl was young, no job, and no ambition whatsoever."

"Let me finish. When a man like your husband cheats after the problems ya'll were having, he wasn't feeling like he was King of his castle. You were beautiful and independent, so he went to where he could feel important. He was King in *her* castle."

"I'm really not feeling what you're saying to me right now."

"I'm not justifying his actions, just trying to put you in his head. Your husband put make-up on her ugly world to make it prettier. She was just a piece of ass to him, but he was probably the best thing in her life. She played her role as the sideline ho. More than likely she cooked for him and got a little more freaky than you would. She was there any time he needed her and he probably talked to her any kind of way and she accepted it because he was giving her money."

"So a man would leave a dime like me to be with a nickel?"

"Not 'be with' ... fuck. There's a difference. He wouldn't be in a committed relationship with her, it would just be about the sex."

"You're starting to make me depressed so now you have to cheer me up."

I kissed her neck and started caressing her breasts. Her body shifted when she felt my manhood poking her back. As she lowered and took me in her mouth, I sat back and closed my eyes. All my troubles seemed obsolete, nothing else mattered, there was no place I'd rather be. It was all about right here, right now.

Dawn got up and went to the bed. She kissed her lover as she quietly slept. Dawn cuddled up next to Tracy and continued kissing and touching her until the sleeping beauty woke up. She woke up with a huge smile, pulled Dawn on top and kissed her with passion. Tracy closed her eyes as if she was thinking my thoughts, enjoying the moment. Tracy opened her eyes again, that's when she looked toward the couch. She smiled. A simple gesture that made me feel good after what Dawn told me about Tracy's past.

Dawn and Tracy locked legs, scissors style, their grind was slow and seductively sexy. Watching these two beautiful women pleasure each other was intoxicating. Their slow grind sped up and the sounds of love making got louder. Tracy was making some serious sex faces as she closed her eyes and tilted her head toward the ceiling. She looked as if she was praying to the sex gods. Tracy had to be thanking them for her feelings of ecstasy and her impending orgasm. Dawn and Tracy came at about the same time.

When they unlocked legs, I went to Tracy and put my tongue deep inside her. She grinded on my tongue as I pulled her body closer by her thighs. Dawn took one of Tracy's breasts in her mouth. Tracy was a loud lover; her moans and groans were muffled because her feet were crossed behind my head. Her legs had my ears covered. She screamed she was about to cum. When her legs locked tighter around my head, she screamed louder, and tried to twist away. But I wouldn't let her go even after she came. Tracy finally wiggled away hyper-ventilating like she was having an asthma attack.

As Tracy tried to gain her composure, I entered Dawn from behind. She arched her back so her ass could be up a little higher. With my hand gripping both sides of her hips, I slowly and steadily pulled her ass back and forth toward me. I closed my eyes, fell into the moment, wishing it could last forever. My Keith Sweat moment was interrupted by the tongue that eased into my mouth. Tracy and I were kissing like teenagers as I continued my in and out motion with her lover.

Dawn stopped my multi-tasking when she took over. She started pushing back and forth harder and faster. Her soft ass slapping against my pelvis sounded like thunder. When she tried to slow down, I grabbed her hips again to keep the pace the same. Tracy sat back to admire the show. She bit her lip as she penetrated her wet spot with her fingers. I felt my volcano about to erupt so I pulled out. I shot my potential children on

Dawn's backside. Tracy came to us and put her fingers in my mouth.

Satisfied and weak, I sucked the wetness off her digits and collapsed in the middle of the bed. The beautiful women in my bed cuddled up beside me on both sides. They met over my chest and kissed each other, and then kissed me.

Silence was in the air as they laid their heads on my chest. I guess the silence meant we were deep in our own thoughts. Their thoughts quickly changed to dreams. As my sleeping beauties slept, all my worries, all my drama and problems were a distant memory.

I was starting to lose my fight with the sandman and I thought, how could my dreams ever be any better than this moment?

DeShon

Fool for Love

The bell rang for school to be out. I was at my desk with the weekend of events fresh on my mind. My closest friends were at each other's throats. I thought they were going to kill each other. There was something in Jason's eyes that I hadn't seen before. He seemed to have some serious hate for Reggie. All the drama with Monica must have him on edge.

With all that mess going on, I didn't get to tell him Nicole was back in town. I called him earlier today and told him to come by the gym to see my new transfer. The news of Nicole would lift his spirits, hell she lifted mine because ultimately it will help me get some info about Tiffany.

Tiffany moved to Texas after high school and had been outta sight, outta mind ever since. Seeing Nicole caused a whole lot of memories to resurface. I screwed up with Tiffany back in the day and never really got any real closure and my love life has been a joke ever since. Tiffany was running through my mind like a gazelle when Jason stuck his head in the door.

"I know that look, you got some chick on your mind. You sprung again?"

"Shut up fool, you don't know me that well."

He chuckled, "Come on D, tell me you weren't thinking about a female just now."

"Don't walk in my office talking shit. By NCAA standards can you even be here? Don't make me drop a dime on you."

"Please, I do everything by the book. And since you avoiding the question I know the answer. We'll talk about the chick on your mind after you show me your new kid."

I got up from the desk and walked past my friend wearing the UALR sweat suit. I grabbed Brandon's jersey and went out on the court. The team was still doing their stretches. I told my regular starters they would be scrimmaging the second team with the new kid running the point. When I handed Brandon his jersey, his face lit up like Christmas lights when he saw the number. I walked back to the sideline where Jason was standing, he still had no idea who Brandon was.

"Which one is the transfer?"

"The kid wearing number 4."

"My Number? Why you do the boy like that? He got big shoes to fill. I still hold the school and conference records for assists and steals. They should retire my number."

"Oh they will, when he's done with it."

My starting point guard was good but he was no Brandon. After about six minutes everyone in the gym knew Brandon was the best player on the floor. My second team never beat the starters in practice but they were nursing an early 10-point lead.

"You were right D; this kid is nice. Where did he come from?"

"Conway."

"Conway, he should have been on my radar. What did you say his name was again?"

"Actually I never told you his name, but if you must know, the kids name is Brandon Dade."

I could tell that name instantly registered in Jason's mind. He focused in on the young man wearing his old jersey. He walked out on the court trying to get a closer look, but the boys were still playing. I called time-out so that this love-sick fool didn't hurt one of my players. They were about to run his ass over. Jason was in a daze staring at Brandon. I told Mike Ford to check in and called Brandon to the sideline.

"Way to play out there son, when you learn the offense, you are going to be a great asset to this team."

I was talking but Jason was just standing there looking crazy like we were playing freeze tag. The boy from his past looked up at him smiled, "Hey Jason, do you remember me?"

I was surprised to know he still knew who Jason was. Then Brandon began telling us about a box of our high school games tapes. He said he watches the tapes all time. He was talking to both of us but his eyes never left Jason. He said he thought we had the best back court in the state that year.

Since my homie was still a mute statue, I told Brandon to go check back in the game. He said ok and started to run back toward the game but he ran up to Jason and hugged him. I didn't think J would hug him back because he was still looking like a mannequin.

Finally, Jason hugged him back and said, "You gotta nice game kid. You doing your thang out there." Brandon let go and ran back to the court smiling like he had just met Michael Jordan.

Steven "Chris" Ware

"You ok bro? Now I gotta use *your* favorite phrase J, what's on *your* mind?"

"Yeah I'm good. But my mind is everywhere. It's crazy cause all the bullshit going on in my life right now is suddenly a distant second to what I'm thinking. At the moment all the good times I had with that boy and his momma is all I can think about."

"Brandon told me about an incident with his sleazy coach over in Conway. That's why he transferred here. He seems like a good kid and he's one helluva ball player. Nicole has done a great job with him. And she was looking great too, by the way."

I looked in his eyes to see his reaction to that statement.

"Wait a minute, you saw Nicole? When? Why the hell are you holding back information?"

I smiled, "Calm down dude, one question at a time. I saw her Friday when she enrolled Brandon in school. I was going to tell you at the fight party but you and Reggie had that bullshit on yall mind."

"You got me there. Was John with them?"

"Who the hell is John?"

"Brandon's daddy, fool."

"Why would I need to remember that nigga's name, fool? But if you must know she was alone. She works at Baptist Memorial and said she is buying a house over in Stone Links."

My cell rang. I answered it and watched J's face. He zoned out again, thinking about his first love.

"Man D, I really wanna see her."

"Well you gonna get your chance. We got to head over to Baptist. That was Johnny, Reggie just got shot."

Jason

A Madhouse

There were so many emotions in my head as we raced down University Avenue toward I-630. My first love was back in town working at Baptist Memorial Hospital. Reggie, my friend since grade school, is at that same hospital with a bullet hole in his chest. We had been friends so long, yet we were almost ready to kill each other just the other night.

DeShon was still on the phone with Johnny getting the details from this morning's events. He was doing his best Jeff Gordon impersonation down one of the busiest streets in Little Rock. The way he was bobbing and weaving through traffic, running red lights, you would think he had a siren and lights flashing on his GMC Denali.

It's strange to feel excitement, sorrow, and guilt all at the same time. The Mayweather fight was almost just an under card bout cause me and Reggie were about to go at it. The beef between us had been brewing for months. He was right, I didn't like his lifestyle. Monica had cheated with someone who was probably like Reggie. I knew the guy's name but never saw his face. Sometimes when the pain and hurt of what she did got the best of me, it was Reggie's face I saw sexing my wife.

Arguing with a person you already have ill feelings toward and liquor is not a good combination in any setting. I don't think we said anything to one another we can't get past. But if we had fought, we wouldn't have gone to the point of no return.

From what I overheard from DeShon's conversation, Reggie had been shot twice. One bullet went in and out, but surgery was needed to remove the other one. I hadn't heard about the who or the why. Reggie could have died without us having a chance to clear the air. I was now about to lose *my* life trying to see *him* because D was on his phone driving like a madman.

He shouldered passed this old couple and scared them half to death when he laid on his horn. I looked back to see if they were ok, and the Mrs. Claus look-a-like on the passenger side gave us the middle finger of hate. I tightened up my seat belt. As we pulled in to the hospital complex, we looked up at each other when we saw all four media outlets on the scene. I'm not a mind reader but he had to be thinking the same thing, Sugar Honey Iced Tea.

Johnny told us to bypass the ER and come up to the third floor where the rest of the family were waiting. We rode the elevator in silence. I was wondering if Reggie's family knew about our confrontation. Some of them may not want me here. We stepped off the elevator, Johnny was outside the waiting room on his cell. He ended his call when he saw us. His eyes were red, worry lines creased his forehead, and he had concern for a cousin who was more like a brother.

"Man I'm happy to see ya'll. It's been a madhouse up here."

I asked, "How is he?"

Before he said anything, he hugged me.

Not a man hug, he hugged me tight and hard. He let go and hugged DeShon the same way. It eased my mind a little and let me know I was welcomed here, at least by him.

Wiping tears from his eyes he said, "Doc said he gon be ok. He's woke. Momma and pop in there with him now. They're the only ones to talk to him so far."

"When we were on the phone you didn't say nothing about all the news vans outside."

"They just got wind of it. Trying to get the top story for the 10 o'clock news I guess."

I asked, "Who else is here?"

"Only Uncle Ray and Aunt Audrey right now." He went on telling us the family members who had been in and out. A lot of family and friends were on the way up there after work. He said his cousins Travis and Sam had already been up talking crazy and ready to 'ride on the nigga who had shot their big cuz.' They were from McAlmont and were some straight up hood niggas, ready to put in work at a moment's notice.

Reggie and Johnny had a big family and we knew all of them. It didn't matter the event: holidays, birthday parties, and reunions, DeShon and I were always invited. We were honorary cousins.

Johnny said, "The dude who shot him is already dead."

"Travis and 'nem got him already? Them niggas off tha chain. What happened?"

"Naw D, dude killed hisself. "

Before he could tell us anymore, his parents came from Reggie's room around the corner. After hugs and greetings, Mrs. Crew looked at me and said, "Reggie wants to see you next."

Jason

Soul Mates

R eggie had been sleeping with Joselyn Greer every Wednesday for the last 3 months. The Greers lived next door to Ms. Lisa Swain, our high school guidance counselor. Ms. Swain was Reggie's first paying customer when he started his landscaping business years ago. He now had a crew working for him but he still always did Ms. Swain's yard himself. He wanted to give her special treatment for encouraging him to pursue his dream.

Joselyn and her husband moved there about a year ago. Joselyn approached Reg one day to inquire about his yard services as a front to give him her number. Turns out she had been admiring him from her window. In the spring and summer months Reg usually works topless or in a tank top. With his lean muscular body, he looks more like a middle weight boxer instead of a gardener, and he loves showing it off.

For the past few months Joselyn and Reg had been rendezvousing in hotels, parks and parking lots to have sex.

He was feeding her hunger for a more exciting sex life.

Reg noticed Joselyn was becoming increasingly clingy but he ignored it, because she was extra fine and the sex was on another level.

Early this morning Reggie was at Ms. Swain's house doing her yard. Joselyn came out of her house and motioned for Reggie to follow her to the back yard. She led him to a tool shed/garage. In the garage was a '64 Chevy Impala that Mr. Greer was restoring. As Joselyn took off her bathrobe, Reggie heard her talking but he wasn't really listening, he was too busy checking out her husband's nice old school ride. If he had been paying attention, he would have heard her say Mr. Greer was in the house asleep.

Joselyn wanted something that she thought only Reggie could provide.

"I need to feel you inside me now," was the last thing he remembered before he raised up her long pearl colored nightgown and gave her what she needed. Reggie and Joselyn bent over the trunk of that classic car and she moaned in pure delight. They both jumped when they heard movement toward the front of the shed.

Mr. Greer was standing there with what looked to be a snub nosed .38 revolver by his side in his right hand. By now Reggie had pulled out and Joselyn was standing up straight. Mr. Greer raised the gun and his eyes and weapon were fixated on Reggie. Reggie said he saw so much anger in Mr. Greer's eyes, and he pleaded with him to stay calm.

Joselyn stepped in front of her lover and begged her husband not to shoot. Reggie watched Mr. Greer's eyes, he saw anger turn to hurt. Mr. Greer fired three shots, turned and walked back toward the house when he saw the bodies hit the ground. He had two bullets left in his gun but he only needed one. Mr. Greer went back to his bedroom, sat down on his wife's side of the bed. He put the gun to his temple and pulled the trigger.

The first shot Mr. Greer fired went through Joselyn's heart into Reggie's abdomen. she was dead before she hit the ground. The other two were aimed at Reggie's chest, both were inches apart striking him in the chest just below his collarbone. That was the story Reggie told me as I sat next to his hospital bed.

"Jason, man I will never forget the look on that man's face when Joselyn stepped in front of that gun. All I wanted to do was get outta there alive. She showed her love for me by trying to save my life and that's sad because I didn't give a damn about her. She was just one of many. That shit is fucking with me dude."

"I can only imagine."

"Look J, the shit I said to you the other night..."

I cut him off and told him this wasn't the time nor the place, we could deal with all that when he was up and out of the hospital. He turned his head towards me to give half a smile, "Nigga, I just looked the grim reaper in the eye and lived to tell about it. Bullets being shot at a nigga's ass got me feeling emotional. So shut up and listen to what I got to say."

I put both hands in the air to surrender, "Go ahead bro. Speak ya mind."

"Back in high school, I was jealous of you, hell everybody was. Nobody hated on you, just wanted what you had with Nicole, you feel me?"

"Kinda."

"J, she was as fine as any chick we had ever seen and you loved her. And despite everything that happened everyone knew she loved you. She was just cool. Y'all were always together but she gave you enough space to hang out with us. We all envied that. Do you remember Michelle Bonds?"

"Of course, she was your first love. She really screwed you over. You were messed up about it. Why you ask me about her?"

"Yeah when I found out she cheated on me with that science nerd it devastated me. But when you and Nicole broke up, I lost faith in love and relationships."

"Wait, science nerd? Wendell Johnson? You never said who she messed around with. Wow. Wendell was super lame back in the day, he..."

Reggie cut me off, "Focus nigga, don't remind me how lame the dude was who fucked Reggie Crew's girl. I'm talking about what started my negative attitude about women and love. Something has gotta change bro cuz I almost died today."

I told him that he and I were at the same crossroad. I told him what I had confessed to Dawn a few nights ago. I told him about all the faceless, nameless sex I'd had over the past few months. If I thought about it a lot harder, I could probably remember a few names and even more faces. But those women mean nothing to me, they started becoming a distant memory when I busted that nut.

"Jason, we messed up in the head my brother. But we ain't too far gone, we have identified the problem and are willing to find a solution. So we good. You are willing to change, right?"

"You think there is rehab for people who like to hit it and quit it?"

"Dude I'm serious."

I smiled, "I'm joking. I can embrace change. This lifestyle we living is lonely and by looking at you, dangerous. No offense."

"None taken, but you can get a head start, the solution to your problem works in this hospital."

"What you mean?"

"Don't play dumb. She was the first face I saw when I woke up from surgery."

"I haven't saw her yet and how you figure she's the solution to my problem."

"Fool because you get a second chance. You single, she's single, and I know this because I asked her already. Seems like you need a bullet in yo behind to give you some clarity cuz you killing me with this stupidity right now."

"I feel you man, I still love her, and I still want her. She might be single, but where is Brandon's dad? I don't know if he's still in the picture."

"Don't worry about all that, everything will work itself out. Nicole is your soul mate, go get her dude. I was the doggiest of all dogs and I believe in love again. I believe we all have a soul mate. Go out there and get yours and tell someone else to come holla at they boy."

"Ok, Ok, I'm out. I'll go find Nicole and talk to her. You get some rest, and Reg?"

"What?"

"The doggiest of all dogs?" He laughed, "Will Smith said that on The Fresh Prince of Bel Aire, don't question it, just go with it."

I matched his laugh, "I don't care who said it, I'm saying you shouldn't have repeated it. That was corny as hell."

DeShon

First Love

I was at Cache Restaurant in the River Market. Sade was playing in the background as I sipped my Long Island Iced Tea. My eyes were back and forth from the digital display on my phone to the analog dial on my Movado watch, I was impatiently waiting for Tiffany. Excitement and nervousness was all over me. It had been almost a decade since I had laid eyes on my first love.

Since Jason and Nicole had gotten back together, I had been pleading with Nicole to get me a sit down with her friend. Tiffany hadn't even wanted to be in the same room with me since we broke up back in high school. It all went down the night we lost the championship our senior year. She didn't even go to the prom because I found someone else to go with.

Nicole called yesterday to tell me that Tiffany would be in town this weekend and had agreed to meet me. I chose Cache because of its laid-back atmosphere, amazing food and stiff drinks. It was an intimate place where we could have an intimate conversation about the past so we could get some much-needed closure.

Tiffany never gave me a chance to explain what happened the night we broke up.

Johnny and Reggie had the house to themselves the weekend we played in the championship. So of course, they threw a party, just about the whole senior class was in that two-story house that night. Even though we had lost the game, the party was on point. By the time I got there my three amigos were already half drunk. We were only 17 or 18, but Reg had a hook up and was able to get two kegs and a case of Smirnoff wine coolers.

Jason was on crutches but was drinking like a sailor. He was standing in front of the stairs that led to the bedrooms talking to a girl I didn't recognize. Jason was propped up on his crutches with a wine cooler in his left hand, he was slurring his words bad. I pointed to the bottle in his hand, "Don't you think you've had enough?"

"Na I'm good, *Moms.* Tonight, I just lost my girl and looking at my foot maybe even my scholarship. I'm just trying to kill some brain cells. Believe me, I'm straight."

"The way you slurring your words, you about to be brain dead while you trying to kill brain cells. You need to slow your roll. Let me take this off your hands."

I reached for the bottle but he snatched it away from me and lost his balance. I tried to grab his arm before he fell too hard. The arm I grabbed was the one holding the bottle. Jason ended up in a seated position on the bottom step but his drink ended up all over my shirt.

"J, are you ok man?"

"Hell naw bro, I'm far from ok. My life is fucked up right now."

"Ok, I get it but the alcohol ain't making it any better. I'm saying this cuz I love you like a brother. You need to get it together, let me help you upstairs."

"You right D, I'm drunk and I really do need to get upstairs my stomach is bubbling."

I looked around for Johnny and Reggie but I didn't see either one. The chick Jason was talking with was still standing here. This groupie must have had it bad for this negro because J was at his worse and she was still here with a star struck gaze in her eye.

"Look sweetheart, do you know either of the guys who is throwing this party?"

"I know Johnny."

"Cool, go find him for me. Tell him DeShon needs his help."

Now she had a worried look in her eyes.

"Is he gonna be ok, I haven't gave him my number yet."

I started to say something bad to this hoodrat but I bit my tongue.

"He'll be just fine if you hurry up and do what I asked."

Reggie walked up just as Jason's groupie ran off toward the kitchen. He was asking a bunch of unnecessary questions. I told him to grab the crutches and follow us up the stairs. The three of us were all the way up the steps when Johnny ran up. Reggie and I were outside the bathroom door while Jason was at the sink calling Ralph and Earl.

Johnny looked distressed, "Shit man, why did y'all stop at the sink. The fool should be over the toilet."

"We were in a hurry, better the sink than all over the floor."

"Look J, Nicole's a good girl and all but don't lose yourself bro. There are way too many hoes downstairs for you to be acting like this. It bothered me at first when that bitch Michelle played me, but I'm over it."

Johnny agreed with his cousin, "Jason the best way to get over somebody is to get on top of somebody else."

Jason wasn't saying anything, he was just staring at the mirror. Reggie headed back downstairs as Jason's stalker came up the steps with Tonya Jamison. Like I said before I didn't recognize the groupie but we definitely knew Tonya. She was one of McClellan's major drama queens. Tonya was always being accused of flirting with or fucking somebody's boyfriend. What makes it worse is that she really looks good, but like Kanye said, "Sometimes the prettiest people do the ugliest things."

She walked up all in my space, "What's up DeShon? This is my cousin Kim. She's into Mr. Jason Hart over there. She told me what happened, so we came to see if he was ok."

I closed the bathroom door to give Jason some privacy. Johnny spoke before I got a chance to, "Ladies I'm sorry but the upstairs area is invitation only, I need y'all to turn around and go back to the party."

Both girls started to make their way down the steps but Tonya kept looking back at me.

"Johnny, I need to raid your closet. Jason spilled his drink all over me."

"That's cool, you know your way around," Johnny said. "I'm gon escort these sistas back to the party then come back to check on J."

I proceeded down the hallway to Johnny's room to find another shirt. After I pulled my wet polo over my head and dropped it on the floor next to his bed, I stood bare chested in front of a full-length mirror hanging on Johnny's closet door. The bedroom door slowly opened behind me, now Tonya Jamison had a reflection in that same mirror.

"Hold up Tonya, I'm changing clothes in here. Close the door." She did what I asked but not what I meant, and stepped inside the door before she closed it.

"I was headed back downstairs and saw you come in here," she said. "I wanna take my clothes off too."

Tonya was wearing a romper. She took the straps off her shoulders and let her one-piece outfit hit the floor.

She was completely naked. The whole scene threw me off guard, no panties, no bra. I didn't even turn around, I watched her from the mirror. Tonya stepped out of her clothes which were now around her ankles and took a step toward me. I couldn't lie and say I wasn't aroused because my soldier was standing at full attention. "Look Tonya, it ain't about to go down like this, my girl will be here any minute."

"Well I see something that's telling me different."

Her eyes were looking down between my legs. Before I could say anything else the reflection in the mirror suddenly became a ménage a trois as Tiffany stepped into the doorway. Tiffany's eyes were wide with disbelief as she moved them back and forth from me to Tonya's bare ass. She didn't say a word as her eyes filled with tears and she ran back towards the stairs. I pushed passed Tonya to chase after Tiffany.

She tried to grab me as I went by, and I heard her say something like, "She's gone now, so what's up?"

By the time I started down the steps, my girl was already out the front door.

I had to look like a topless madman the way I was moving. When I made it to the front porch, I slowed down to see which direction Tiffany had gone. She was almost two blocks down the street to my left but she was no longer running. Tiffany was walking at a determined pace like Jason Voorhees or Michael Myers. I took off in a sprint in her direction, she had already started her car by the time I reached her.

"Look it's not what it looks like, nothing happened. Let me explain." I was out of breath.

"It was about to happen though right? Both of y'all in there naked, what you gotta explain?"

"Open the door, it's only a misunderstanding. Just calm down, let me tell you what happened."

"Don't freakin tell me to calm down you cheating bastard. Back away from my car before I run your ass over."

She was parallel parked and she had to back up a little bit to get out. When she pulled away from the curb she almost side swiped me. Tiffany sped back towards the house and double parked in front of it. She jumped out of her car and went back into the house. I hope she wasn't about to fight with Tonya. I ran toward the house but when I got there, Tiffany and her cousin Jazmine were walking to the car. I called out for Tiffany but she didn't even look up. I guess Jazz had been quickly debriefed because she glanced at me with two fingers up, and they weren't her thumbs. They got into the car and sped off.

As I slowly walked back to the house, a few people had gathered on the porch hoping to see drama. Tonya was one of them. My mind was on finding a shirt to put on and whether or not I was gonna punch this bitch Tonya in her face.

I was shaken from that unpleasant memory as I saw Tiffany walk into the restaurant. Since I was facing the entrance, I saw her walk up to the hostess stand.

It was nearly 7:15.

I stood up at our table so she could see me. This Nubian goddess moved through the room like she owned it. Cache was now her own super model runway.

I'm just guessing but everything she had on looked expensive. She wore a sexy red dress that was probably Donna Karen, a pair of 9" heels with soles that were the same color as her dress, all accentuated with a Dooney & Bourke clutch bag. Class and style was all over her. I was just standing there thinking to myself, "Damn she still look good, don't F it up."

Tiffany's shoulder length dreadlocks were a surprise to me though, since last time I saw her she didn't have them. When she got to the table I thought about reaching out to hug but I didn't want to over step my bounds. So instead I extended my arm for a handshake, "It's great seeing you Tiffany, you look amazing."

"Good Evening Mr. Bryson, sorry I'm late. I had a hard time finding a parking space." She barely touched my hand as she sat down. I guess calling me Mr. Bryson was her way of keeping this as impersonal as possible. The waitress showed up when I sat down so we ordered a couple of drinks. Tiffany ordered a glass of white wine, I got another beer.

"Look Tiffany, I've asked you here to discuss the past. I just need some closure. I know it's been at least 7 years but you never gave me a chance to explain. Honestly I still have feelings for you."

"Feelings for me? What could you possibly be feeling for me Mr. Bryson? That was high school, a lifetime ago."

"I don't know what these feelings are, but it's something. I do know that since you I haven't had any meaningful relationships. I haven't felt anything for anybody like the feelings I had for you."

"That was high school puppy love. But it makes sense now, this must be part of your therapy. Which step is this in your recovery? The step when you have to apologize to all the hearts you've broken?"

Tiffany took a sip of her wine. She had no smile, and no frown. She was trying her best to act like she was in control, but she kept shifting in her seat. She was nervous. I asked her to hear me out so I could explain my side of the story. She went off.

"Ok, go ahead. But I'll tell you now it won't change anything. All I know is that I get to the party, Reggie tells me you are upstairs where I find my man in a room half naked with a girl who is completely naked. Not just any girl but the neighborhood hoe. The bitch who was voted most likely to be somebody's piece. Explain how I was supposed to be cool with that, DeShon. Please fucking explain that to me."

Tears were in her eyes, hostility was in her voice and stress was all in her face. I couldn't hold it in any longer, I told her the whole story. I told her everything that happened from the time I walked into that house until she opened the door to Johnny's room. When I stopped talking, we sat there with an awkward silence for what seemed like an eternity.

Tiffany took a few more sips of her wine before she spoke, "So if that's true, why in the world would you take her to the prom? That was tacky to say the least."

"In hindsight, I can agree it was tacky. I made a poor decision, I was 17. The prom was a few weeks after that night. I didn't wanna go by myself. She made herself available."

"DeShon, you didn't have to go at all. I didn't. You turned her down that night but you definitely had sex with her prom night. Sex with her was something you must have been longing for."

"Whoa, who told you that? Tonya and I didn't do anything prom night."

"Don't deny it. She went on and on about your night together at graduation rehearsal. The sound of her voice made me nauseous, and the stuff she was saying you guys did made it worse."

"Tiffany, let me say this loud and clear: I. Have. Never. Slept. With. Tonya. Jamison. Never. She was more of a drama queen than I thought. I was a miserable date, still messed up about you. We didn't even dance together. After we took pictures, I dropped her off at the post prom party and went home."

"So basically you're telling me I've been mad at you all these years for nothing."

"I wouldn't say nothing. It was a misunderstanding. It did look bad, it looked really bad. But you were so hurt and upset, you avoided me. You wouldn't even take my phone calls."

"Well DeShon, I think I owe you an apology."

"No apology is needed. But I will say this, like Jason and Nicole, a second chance has presented itself to us. I think we should give love another try."

I extended my arm and hand across the table towards her. She didn't say a word, she just closed her eyes and exhaled as she reached out for my hand.

Nicole

In A Bad Place

A s soon as I walked in from work, I headed straight for my bathtub. I turned the hot water on, lit my candle and went to the fridge to get the bottle of Moscato Rubino. It was a Thursday night and I had the weekend off. I quickly got out of my work scrubs and put on Jason's robe. The past few months have been surreal, Jason Hart was back in my life and had already started leaving clothes at my home.

I haven't been this happy in years. Jason is an awesome man, and Brandon loves him to death. Jason spends just as much time with Brandon as he does with me. And I don't mind that at all. Basketball season is over but J picks my son up from school most days and they go to the gym at UALR to workout. Brandon has even tagged along with Jason on a few of his recruiting trips. On my last weekend off a couple of weeks ago, Jason introduced us to Niya. I was really nervous about it but even that went well. She is adorable. Jason says she is already asking to go back to see her big brother. Everything seems like a fairy tale right now.

I had a big smile on my face as I was thinking about my life.

I turned the water off and poured myself a glass of wine. Just when I was about to slide out of my robe the doorbell rang.

My first thought was that it was Jason and Brandon. Sometimes they ring the doorbell when Jason has takeout, their hands are usually too full to stick the key in the door. The doorbell chimed again when I was a few steps from the door, these two are so impatient.

I opened the door, but it wasn't my men. It was John, Brandon's father. I forget all fairy tales have some form of evil in the story.

John Buckner was at my door in a military uniform. I was standing there wearing nothing but my boyfriend's robe. "What are you doing here?"

"Sorry to show up unannounced, I had a hard time trying to track you guys down. May I come in?"

"Whatever you have to say, you can say it right here. And be sure to say it fast, I want you gone before my son gets home."

"Honestly, I just came to talk to our son. I'm being deployed to Afghanistan. I'm trying to get some things off my chest. Please hear me out."

Against my better judgment, I stepped aside to let him in. I closed the door, and made sure my robe was secure. At that moment I was glad I had on Jason's big robe.

"Since we're being honest, Brandon will not want to hear anything you have to say. He has some for real hatred for you. What can you possibly have to say after all this time?"

"I can't do anything about the past. I'm just trying to deal with the present and the future if that's possible. I want my wife and my baby boy to have a relationship with my son."

I glanced down at the gold band on his left hand, "Your wife? When did you get married?"

"Got hitched about 18 months ago."

That news kind of stung. John had never even mentioned marrying me. He went on to tell me how after he left the last time, his weed and liquor addiction had gotten worse. He was in a bad place so he detoxed a couple of days and then enlisted into the Army. After boot camp he was stationed at Ft. Bliss in El Paso, Texas. That's where he met his wife. They have a baby boy who will be a year old next month. A month after his son's birthday his unit will be headed to the Middle East.

"It's good to hear you finally got your life together John but what do you have to say to Brandon?"

"Well since I've had a steady income the military has been taking money from my check for him but I didn't know where to have the money sent. And like I said, I can't change the past. I just need to tell my son face to face that I'm sorry and that I'm a changed man. I want and need to have some kind of relationship with him."

"And like I said Brandon is very bitter about you. We need to proceed with caution."

"I know a lot has happened, I'm just going to leave my information. This is my cell number and home address in El Paso. Also on here is the hotel where I'm staying and the room number. I'll be here until Monday. I'd really like to speak to him before I leave."

Just as he handed me the folded sheet of paper, Jason and Brandon walked in.

Damn!

Jason

Forever yours

I pulled in to Nicole's driveway and parked beside a rented sedan. The Chevy Malibu had a Hertz sticker on the license plate. Brandon and I had just finished playing some pickup games at the Bill Harmon Rec Center across town in Sherwood. I was in sweaty gym clothes, ready to hit the shower so I wasn't prepared to meet and greet company. But I was cool with it because I was happy. I looked down at the keys in my hand. I had keys to Nicole's home, her car and the invisible key to her heart. I was proud to be a part of her life again. I was a part of their lives and they were at part of mine. Niya had met Nicole and Brandon. My daughter was already calling Brandon her big brother. Everything was going great.

I got to the front door and it was already unlocked. Nicole was in the living room wearing my bathrobe. John was standing across from her in an Army uniform. My hands instantly became sweaty and heart was pounding like I was still running up and down that court. John's face was wearing a nervous smile when he looked at Brandon and spoke to him. His smile faded when he looked up and saw me. The last time we were in the same living room, I whipped his ass. The look on his face told me he remembered.

"What the hell is he doing here?" Brandon was talking to his mom but he never took his eyes off John. Brandon had his basketball under his left arm. His right arm was bouncing back and forth against his leg and his hand was in a fist.

"Brandon watch your mouth and please calm down. Your daddy just needs to talk to you about a few things."

"Son, I just need a little time to explain a few things. It took me awhile to find you guys."

"Find us? We just moved here a few months ago. The rest of the damn time we were in the same place you left us at!"

"Brandon, this is your last warning. That is no way to talk to your father."

"Really Ma? First you said my daddy. Now you just called him my father. This nigga is dead to me. The last time I saw him, he was punching and kicking you in the face. This some bullshit."

In the blink of an eye, Brandon was out the front door. Nicole headed towards the door franticly calling for her son to come back. John's feet were in cement as he looked up at me. But I turned to chase after my woman. Nicole was in the driveway and almost in the road calling for Brandon but he was already halfway across the field on the other side of the street. When I saw that he still had his ball I knew where he was going.

"Pump your brakes baby, you don't have any clothes on. He's headed to the basketball court on the other side of that field. I'll go get him."

Steven "Chris" Ware
249

"I knew he wasn't ready to see John but I didn't think he would run off." She grabbed me in an embrace. "Jason go get my baby, please bring my baby back."

She was crying hysterically. I kissed on her on the forehead then jumped in the truck and headed for the basketball court. When I parked and walked toward the court, no one was out there but Brandon, who was in the middle of the court sitting on his basketball. By the time I stepped on the court he had stood up and started shooting at the basket farthest from me.

"Let go son, I'm here to take you back."

"Is he still there?" He was shooting. He was making every shot he threw up.

"Not sure but probably so."

"Well I ain't going back till he's gone."

"Look man, your mom is worried. She is back there crying like crazy. Nicole said he wants to talk, so just listen to what's on his mind and maybe he'll be on his way."

He stopped shooting and looked up at me. "Why in the hell would I listen to anything he has to say?"

"Brandon, you have a real reason to be upset and confused, but you're being really disrespectful. Your mouth is outta control right now."

"I'm sorry Mr. J but I don't have any words for that dude. You have been more of a father to me than he has."

"And you know what no one is asking you to say anything. Just listen to what he has to say. At the end of the day that man is your father. You know I don't want him around for selfish reasons but he is your dad Brandon and whether he's in your life or not, I'm not going anywhere. At least do it for your mother, she is freaking out."

"You gonna stay while I talk to him?"

I looked over my shoulder like I was making sure no one was behind and whispered to him, "As long as that ninja is there, I'll be there," I said that with a wink.

Brandon smiled and we piled into my ride to head back to the house. The rental was still in the driveway when we got back. Nicole must have been in the window because she was running toward us before he got out of the truck. I guess she put her work clothes back on because she was wearing a pair of scrubs.

Nicole almost tackled Brandon when she got to him. She had the boy in a bear hug as she kissed his cheek repeatedly.

"Please Brandon don't ever run off like that again. You had me so worried. If you don't want to listen to what your fa...I mean John has to say, I won't make you. Just don't ever run off like that again."

"Ok mama, you're choking me."

She loosened her grip on him a little and wiped the tears from her cheeks as she continued to kiss his.

"I'm sorry baby, you got your mama's pressure up."

"No ma it's me who needs to apologize, I shouldn't have reacted that way. And I shouldn't have been cursing like that. I was out of line. Mr. J talked me into going back to at least listen to what he has to say."

Nicole hugged and kissed him one more time. She looked up at me and smiled, "Well I'm glad Mr. J was here. Go inside and talk to John, Jason and I will be right out here."

Brandon took a few steps toward the front door but then he turned to run in my direction and gave me a big hug before going into the house. When he was out of sight Nicole walked up to me and grabbed both my hands. She stared deep in to my eyes, "I'm going inside to get cleaned up, when they get done talking we're going to go out to dinner."

"You, Brandon and John?"

"No silly. You, me and Brandon. I can only imagine what you're thinking about all this drama. I made the wrong decision when I chose John over you all those years ago. I should have known then what I know now, you are my soul mate. If you'll have me, I'm yours forever."

I pulled her closer to me and said, "I can dig being your soul mate. And forever? I can definitely get with that."

Nicole

Before I Let Go

I was standing in the mirror with a towel wrapped around my body. I was admiring my makeup. Makayla Smith, one of DeShon's cousins, had done my face and Tiffany's a few hours ago. My ego was beaming with pride because I really liked the reflection I was looking at. MaKayla had done an amazing job. Jason and DeShon had something cooked up for me and Tiffany. We both had hair and nail appointments earlier today. When I got back from the beauty shop, Jason had a sexy red evening gown on my bed. Also there was a box of Jimmy Choo's on the floor at the foot of the bed. A bouquet of white roses was on my dresser. The note in the flowers read:

Be ready @ 7:30. I love you!

Neither of us had any clue what was going on. All the mystery was so exciting. Let me hurry up and get ready before time gets away from me. It was already 6:30. I was checking myself in my full-length mirror when my doorbell rang. The red numbers on the digital clock on my night stand read 7:28. This beautiful off the shoulder dress fit me perfectly. I checked my makeup for the umpteenth time before I walked to the door. When I opened my front door, there was a man standing there in a black suit. Behind him was a black limo parked at the end of my driveway. "Hello Ms. Dade, I will be your driver this evening. Are you ready to leave?"

I told him yes and he escorted me to the car. He opened the door for me and I climbed in. Tiffany was seated in the back of the limo with a wide-eyed grin. "Nicole, girl can you believe all this? I'm ecstatic right now."

"Me too. Girl that dress is bad ass. You look gorgeous." Tiffany's dress was sky blue and strapless. She was sitting but she still looked like a super model.

"This dress and heels were wrapped in boxes on my bed when I got home. It's like Christmas in the spring at my place."

I told her about how my dress and shoes had a similar story. We talked and laughed as we were chauffeured to our mystery location. It was great having her back in Arkansas full time.

Tiffany moved back home because her and DeShon were back together. The distance from here to Texas was too much. Both of them were beating up the highway trying to spend as much time together as possible. DeShon applied for jobs in Dallas, and Tiffany applied for jobs here. She got a call back first, so now she's back home for good. I love seeing my friend happy. DeShon has been spoiling her rotten. Not just with gifts but with most of his time. I guess he's trying to make up for lost time. They make a beautiful couple, I'm happy for my friend.

Tiffany and I stopped talking for a second so we could look out the window to try to guess where we were headed. At the moment we were exiting the expressway at Broadway. We had been traveling on I-630. We seemed to be headed downtown. The limo made a right on Markham and turned into the Marriot

Hotel. Our driver got out to open our door. After he helped each of us out of the car, he tipped his hat and told us to enjoy the rest of the evening. I turned to face the hotel. Jason and DeShon walked out of the hotel wearing tuxedos with bowties and vests that respectively matched our dresses

"Jason, baby what is all this?" He walked up to me and gave me a corsage. DeShon had one for Tiffany as well.

"Well ladies on behalf of DeShon and myself we would like to welcome you to the prom. We all missed out on going to the prom, so we put our heads and resources together and tonight we are going upstairs to relive our prom."

I was speechless. When I looked at Tiffany she was crying. She grabbed a hold of DeShon and started kissing him like she was never gonna see him again.

"Dang Tiffany ease up on my homie, we going upstairs to the ballroom not to one of the bedrooms."

"Jason leave them alone. Come here and kiss me like that. You really know how to take care of your woman, this is wonderful."

He did as he was told. After he kissed me, the four of us went inside to take an elevator ride to the 8th floor. When we walked into the ballroom there were about 100 people spread around the room. Some were at the bar, some were sitting down eating but most were on the dance floor.

"Before I Let Go" by Frankie Beverly and Maze was blaring through the speakers.

"Oh my God Nic, look at Brandon. He looks so handsome." That was Tiffany.

I scanned the room in the direction she was looking and saw my baby boy in a suit and tie. He was the one playing the music. "Jason how did you get my son to wear a suit? I can't believe this."

"I didn't know he hated dressing up, I had to promise him tickets to a Memphis Grizzles game when they play his team."

"Getting him to wear a button-down shirt is like pulling teeth, so I know you had to promise him something big to get him to wear a suit and tie."

Before I started mingling with the other guests, I went over to talk to my son. He had been receiving and sending letters from John since he had been deployed. Brandon and John were in an ok place. I'm glad too. I didn't want my son growing up with all that hate in his heart. He was excited to one day meet his little brother.

"Hey Mr. DJ. What you know about Frankie Beverly?"

He smiled, "Hey ma, Mr. J made me a playlist but I actually have a lot of this music on my iPod. I get my taste in music from you. Were you surprised?"

"Yes. I had no idea he was planning all this. I love it."

"Well go enjoy yourself, I'm ok over here."

I made a silly face at him as I walked away, "I'll leave you to it then."

I looked around the room and saw so many familiar faces. Reggie was here with one of my coworkers. They have been dating since he left the hospital after he was shot. They seemed to be getting along ok. Johnny was here as well. Like always he had a BBW by his side. Jason and DeShon were talking to a couple I didn't recognize. I stared at Jason from across the room. I love that man so much. He really is my soul mate.

For a long time, the idea of a soul mate seemed unreal to me. I thought that too many people die lonely for soul mates to exist. But most of the time we run our soul mate off because we don't realize it when they're right in front of us. I almost ran away from my soul mate. But Jason Hart is mine forever. He was walking my way and I couldn't help but smile.

I instantly started crying as he stood there in front of me. I was crying tears of joy, because when he got to me, he went down on one knee with a small box in his hand.

Book Club Discussions

In your opinion, what is a soul mate? Do you think a person only has one?

What could Jason have done differently in regards to Nicole?

What could DeShon have done differently in regards to Tiffany?

Is sex on the first date ok? Does that make you a *hoe* or a *hoodrat*?

"A man will use a woman to feel like the king of his castle, but he won't necessarily make that woman his queen." What are your thoughts?

Why do you think John changed for his wife, but wouldn't change for Nicole?

Should John's son give his father another chance?

DeShon made matters worse by taking the girl he'd gotten caught with to the prom. Why do you think he did that? In a relationship, can the appearance of an indiscretion do as much harm as actually being unfaithful?

Should you give up so easily if the situation doesn't seem 'right'?

Have you been intimate with anyone who has left an article of clothing on during sex? Did it bother you then? Would it bother you now after reading this story?

Is it a good idea to guard your heart? Why or why not? Have you had to guard yours?

How important is status when you're dating? Would you date a man/woman who doesn't have a car or a job? Why or why not?

How often do you think that trouble in relationships are caused by things that happened in a person's past?

About the Author

Author Steven Christopher Ware Sr., AKA *Chris*, proudly states that he was born and raised in Arkansas. Originally from the McAlmont area, he now resides in Sherwood with his beautiful wife Brandi. He has three wonderful children: Jalen (Chelsea), Kasi, and Steven Jr., AKA *C.J.* Chris has been an employee at UPS for almost 25 years.

Black Butterfly Books

is an imprint of

The Butterfly Typeface Publishing.

Books to intelligently entertain
the discriminating reader!

Contact us for all your

publishing & writing needs!

Iris M Williams
PO Box 56193
Little Rock AR 72215